T0131488

ASPEN AND EL REY DE PATAGONIA

DUNCAN CULLMAN

authorHOUSE®

AuthorHouse™
1663 Liberty Drive
Bloomington, IN 47403
www.authorhouse.com
Phone: 1 (800) 839-8640

Published by AuthorHouse 04/15/2020

ISBN: 978-1-7283-5877-2 (sc)
ISBN: 978-1-7283-5872-7 (hc)
ISBN: 978-1-7283-5876-5 (e)

Library of Congress Control Number: 2020906541

Print information available on the last page.

CONTENTS

ASPEN 1971-1974

WAS HITCHHIKING UP Starwood Drive to Spider Sabich's house; I am not sure why. Maybe I thought I could break the ice with him or learn about his training techniques. An old red jeep stopped to give me a ride, as I was still young and innocent looking. It turned out to be a songwriter, John Hicklehooper or some German name, who lived up there and was on his way home. He wore big, thick glasses and said he had moved to Aspen from Denver. He wanted to interview me to find out about all the young people like me who were moving to Colorado to live in its snowy mountains.

So I spilled my story about having left home young and not attending college, working odd jobs, and falling in love with college-bound young ladies, only to become heartbroken as they ditched me for scholars from loving families. I talked about ski racing and Bob Beattie, who had founded the International Pro Ski Racers Association, which was now the new game in town and catching attention from the press nationally and perhaps in northern Europe, where skiing had deeper roots. He was an intelligent fellow, this Schicklgruber, and maybe he sympathized with me as a refugee from a broken past in a less-friendly state way out east where he had never been.

I told him I wanted to live up at the tree line and build a cabin so that my fiancée, who had run off, could possibly come back to visit me, although he sensed realistically that this would never happen. She was a young, talented piano player whose mother had asphyxiated herself in the garage, where the father, a postal delivery man, found her lifeless. So he had raised both children by himself. He didn't like Jews or Negroes, and he was half German, half Scotch. The young girl, barely eighteen, had climbed onto my motorcycle and come to my dormitory, where I had lit a joint and seduced her. However, her mother's ghost had kept reappearing to warn her of my evil intentions, which were not innocent, boyish fantasies but masculine, adult dominance. Perhaps at eighteen she had been still too young to fall in love, or perhaps it had been the reappearing ghost?

The songwriter with the thick glasses interviewed two more refugees like myself and then wrote his next hit song, "Rocky Mountain High," by John Denver, his stage name.

Spider Sabich was not home, but the door was answered by a woman named Claudine Longet, who spoke with a European accent but was polite and good-looking. It was quite a nice house, and I wondered just how he could have paid for it with his ski victories, which had added up to just over $26,000. But maybe it was her house too. Bob Beattie, Sabich's sports agent on the side, landed him a lucrative ski contract with K2 Skis from Vashon Island, Washington, owned by Chuck Ferries, a former US national slalom champion and Olympian.

I hitchhiked down Starwood Mountain to find John Stirling smoking in his Porsche with his three Labradors passed out in the back seat, all stoned. John had been my ski buddy in Portillo several years earlier, but now, after a terrible divorce, he had met a new girlfriend named Ruthie, who was from Pennsylvania.

This was going to put a damper on our relationship, although his other ski race buddy, Jamie Arnold, told me that I could stay over in the original log cabin up there on Missouri Heights in Carbondale, just forty miles from Aspen. John's parents, from Florida, had bought a modest few hundred acres there with their hard work as archaeologists who basically had worked themselves to death renovating San Francisco apartments and Florida land, then died young, leaving John more than four million dollars plus real estate, which back then was a lot of money. John, who was talented, subdivided and built gorgeous dream homes. No wonder Ruthie had found her match. They had three daughters in four years.

Jamie Arnold had a young wife, Colleen, but she had run off for two days to do cocaine with Spider Sabich's brother. That ended the marriage, because Jamie was a bit of a Denver redneck from a poor Irish carpenter father and a headstrong mother, an immigrant with some Scottish nobility in her blood.

In retrospect, I speculate that Spider, who majored in business at the University of Colorado with less-than-average grades, was talked into owing quite a large sum of money, which is called leverage. His brother, however, at least had a pilot's license. Their father was the sheriff in Kyburz, California, and covered for them when and if they got into any scrapes like with Colleen.

So Spider's brother, it was heavily rumored, was flying quite often to Mexico, where he would buy bales of the precious green stuff, then fly to Aspen and toss out the green bales before landing. Or maybe he just landed under police protection? I do not know and have no accurate information.

A deal in Mexico had gone badly, and it was rumored that they lost all their cash, which of course probably meant some of Claudine's cash too. So Spider told Claudine that it was all over, everything. He was going to the airport to fly away for a week, and before he got back, she had better move out of the house. Claudine was the Christmas carol singer Andy Williams's ex-wife. Spider went to the Aspen airport, which was closed because of wind, so he headed home to Starwood.

Several weeks earlier, he had been teaching Claudine how to shoot a gun, in case there was ever a problem with intruders—which most naive, innocent people have no reason to fear in a rich neighborhood of a ski mecca like Aspen.

"Claudine, I told you to be out of here before I returned!" he yelled.

Bang, bang, bang! answered the .22 semiautomatic rifle. Her diary explained everything to the police, who confiscated it without a search warrant after finding Spider's dead body. One bullet had shattered the main artery of his left thigh, causing him to bleed to death within fifteen minutes.

"The diary is inadmissible," declared the court district judge in Aspen. Claudine received three weeks in jail instead of thirty years. After being released, she ran away with her defense lawyer, who left his wife and three children for her.

There was a great, sad memorial for Spider Sabich, who had been the great pro ski champion of that decade. No subsequent pro ski champions ever had his charisma and charm. He had blue eyes like a Siberian Husky, suggestive of something untamable and wild, such as a Siberian wolf. His mother was Russian, and his father, the cop, was Serbian American.

There were a lot of characters in those days in Aspen, before big money came to town. The fact that it was arriving in plenty made some people do even lawless things to pay off mortgages. It's a hard, cold, cruel world out there, but sometimes we have fantasies—the US Ski Team, for instance, which is really just a dream unconnected to any reality, it seems.

John Denver asked his two houseguests, Kellogg Boynton and Steve Douglass, if he could invite me over for a week or two, but they responded that I was way too crazy. "No, no, no!"

A few years later, John Denver took off in his small Cessna without refueling it in California and died in the subsequent plane crash.

THE KING OF
PATAGONIA AND TALES
ARGENTINE AND TALL

El Rey de Patagonia: Part One

(The faraway king of Patagonia, which lies
in southern, far south Argentina?)

WHEN I WAS A SMALL CHILD IN KINDERGARTEN, JUST LEARNING
my ABCs, my teacher read aloud to my entire class, all of
us patiently listening and yawning: "Once upon a time,
a boy dreamed that one day he would become the king of a faraway
kingdom in a distant land."

The idea must have remained latent in the back of my mind,
possibly because I lived in a small house with small parents and yet I
was growing quickly with large feet, hands, and ears. It was obvious that
someday I would become tall, and of course I had large buckteeth. My
parents were upper-lower class: my father was a clerk in a grocery store,
while my mother worked in the Empanadas de Mamy, los Mejores del
Mundo. It was hoped that I, too, would someday be a clerk, but I had
other dreams.

I wanted to be a king. I dreamed of riding a large white horse and carrying a shield and sword. I dreamed of living in a castle. I would go forth and conquer!

My parents finally explained to me that they had adopted me from an orphanage. As an infant, I had been abandoned on the steps of a church. No one knew exactly where I had come from, but a large American car had been seen speeding away.

My mother spoke quietly to calm my fear of the unknowable and unobtainable. "My son, you came directly from God—*El Dios*," she said, for she was Spanish, from some island in the Caribbean. She had gone to Cartagena, in Colombia, to marry my father, but then they had returned to south Bogota, where his parents lived near Portal del Sur of the TransMilenio—although in those days there was no TransMilenio. There are many shops there now, and everyone still rides bicycles. But nowadays there are many more cars, especially from the northern suburbs where the rich live—a lot of Europeans and *gringos Norteamericanos*. My mother had said to me, "Maybe you are one of those gringos, because your hair is blond and your eyes are blue!" We had both laughed.

So I continued to dream that I was destined to be like a king or one of those rich gringos and live in a big mansion with a large garden, many fine trees, and servants that I would treat well since I could identify with them because of my humble origins. My father, though, continued to beat me up when my grades in school were less than good and my teacher would write, "Perhaps your child suffers from schizophrenia, because always he is daydreaming as though in some faraway land."

Because I failed in school, I was sent to work for a man who owned a fleet of bicycle taxis. I was then just fourteen years old and living in what is now known as Porto del Sur ... but back then we called it Bolivar City.

My father kicked me out of the house because of his quarreling with my mother and drinking of chicha, smoking cigars, and gambling away his money on lost causes and the like. He was fighting with my mother and beating her, so I attempted to intervene and was shown out the door.

My pay was not good, barely enough to eat and little left for rent, so I thought I would save some money by sleeping under a bridge or in an arroyo tunnel. I had to build some equity to buy a bus ticket to some better faraway place!

Perhaps I would be a bicycle taxi-man there and make better wages in Madrid or San Francisco or Tokyo or China or London or Rome, or … well, somewhere I would be discovered by an angel whom I might betroth.

I finally settled on the idea of moving to the United States (*Estados Unidos*), where I was promised a job with smugglers of the cocaine plant. I would work on a boat destined for the Yucatan Peninsula from Barranquilla, so I took the bus there to arrive at the appropriate time.

But when the bosses saw me, the whole game plan changed. "You look like a gringo with your *rubio* [blond] hair and your *azul* [blue] eyes. You might be useful to us if you can speak English."

My mother and grandmother had taught me some English, as my grandmother had come from Jamaica, but my accent was bad. Nonetheless, those bosses decided to send me to night class in English to teach me the correct accent. During the day I loaded yachts with big white bags full of *el dorado* (the gold), but I don't think it was gold.

Finally my class ended and I could talk like a Brit, and so my ship came in and off we sailed to the Yucatan, Cancun, or somewhere. But we never landed there and went much farther than that, changing ships midocean, and then someone said, "Look, *Nueva York!*"

I could see the Statue of Liberty. The plan was for me to go through Customs with some rather large bags, like a rich gringo tourist, and the Customs agents had been paid not to bust me and send me to jail for life. It seemed risky to me, so when we passed that Statue of Liberty, I felt like an eagle and jumped overboard.

I could hear some yelling, an alarm, and then gunshots. Bullets ripped into the water around me, and I felt hot in my shoulder, but I am a good floater. The current carried me to some floating garbage, which I clung to, and at dawn I awoke—by the grace of God—on some beach! Luckily it was summer in North America or I would have died of exposure. There was a policeman, then two, strolling the beach, so I crawled into some tall reeds to lie low. Seeing some dogs approaching, I crept into the trees in a neighborhood where school buses were coming for the children, and then I continued into a park to sit upon a bench.

Suddenly a woman jogged by, and seeing me, she screamed in Spanish.

"I am your countryman!" I replied.

"No, I don't think so," she exclaimed, "because your accent is not Mexicano." But noticing my bleeding shoulder, she added, "You are wounded. Have you been shot? And your clothes are disgusting."

She then tore off the lower half of her T-shirt to make a bandage and said, "Should I call for an ambulance or the police?"

"No, no," I protested, adding, "I just came in from the ocean like a fish!"

"Well then, come with me to my brother's house. Maybe he will know what to do."

In my delirium, I thought, *Maybe this is the queen of my future kingdom of North America, the one I am to marry.* But it turned out that she was already married to some local crime boss.

Eventually she actually did lend me enough money to buy some forged documents. They had just killed someone whom nobody would miss, disposing of the body out in the ocean for the sharks to feast on, so all they needed to do was change the picture on the New Jersey driver's license. But, of course, my papers said I was a *Puerto Riqueño* from Ponce, isla Puerto Rico.

Thus I arrived in North America like so many other people of Spanish origin from the south. I even had an accident at my factory job and cut off the tip of my index finger to collect workers' compensation and disability.

Whenever I met my fellow Puerto Ricans, I would ask them about my homeland. They always replied that my accent was more like that of a Spaniard, and I would reply, "Yes, my parents took me to Spain when I was very young," which seemed to make them even more bewildered.

For obvious reasons, I moved from New York to Los Angeles where Puerto Ricans were scarcer. There I was encouraged, because of my good looks, to try out for a backup part in an Arnold Schwarzenegger movie about Colombian drug smuggling, and much to my surprise, I was chosen for a speaking role as a supporting actor playing a Colombian drug smuggler.

Arnold Schwarzenegger was so impressed by my acting abilities that he kindly showed his concern that I not be extradited back to Puerto Rico.

"Thank you so much, Arnold," I said. "Because it has been so long since I've lived there, it might seem like a foreign country."

With a wink, he laughed and told me that he had been born in Austria and that his father had been an SS officer in the Reich. Did I know who my ancestors were? I could probably look them up on ancestry.com.

"Very interesting," I replied, adding that as a child I had often dreamed of being a king in some faraway land like America.

This made him laugh even more, and I was sent to audition for a movie in which I played a crazy attorney named Oreile-Antoine de Tounen, a Frenchman from Chile who proclaimed himself the king of Patagonia, a New France. The Chilean government and the governor of Buenos Aires, Argentina, both sent their armies to arrest de Tounen and have him imprisoned and exiled back to France at various times between 1858 and 1876, whereupon the Argentines promptly occupied the short-lived Arucanian Mapuche Kingdom in Patagonia and annexed that worthless windswept desert for fear that the dreaded English might occupy it and attack Buenos Aires, as they had in 1807.

El Rey de Patagonia: The King of Patagonia was filmed on location in Buenos Aires and Patagonia itself, in Bariloche and San Martin de Los Andes, near many lakes full of salmon and trout, which is called *trucha*—a word for sketchy, undesirable people in Argentina—while I dined on venison stew every other night while on set there. Because of various issues concerning my US passport, I applied for permanent residency, but I was told it was a long process of at least three to six years to become a full Argentine citizen. At least I could obtain a green card and work to support myself while earning meager kickbacks from my movie career everywhere. I was beginning to at least *live* like a king, thanks to the real king, God.

I decided to take a part in a controversial movie about Nazis living in post–World War II Argentina, and was given the role of U-boat captain. In the movie, I arrive in Buenos Aires with a shipment of gold and become one of several trustees to a large Buenos Aires trust fund, but one by one we are murdered—poisoned, shot—by Sicilian "La

Boca" hit men hired by Juan Peron, that famous general-president who married Eva (Evita) Duarte, the blond actress.

It was decided before completion that a lot more music should be added, so in the movie I had to sing that I am a tragic figure whose heart has become truly Argentine, and that I want to abandon the gold and former Nazi ways to become a suave tango dancer instead of a U-boat captain. But I am murdered anyway, for my past sins cannot be forgiven after all, at least not by Juan Domingo Peron and the Argentine treasury.

Argentina decided that my origins were a bit sketchy, and while they didn't exactly call me a *trout* to my face, the office of immigration decided I should return to Puerto Rico, which might claim me because of my large Swiss bank account. This was necessary for my own safety, plus people in Argentina thought that I had actually been brought there in a U-boat and raised in a German conclave in Bariloche by war criminal parents. So much for blond hair and blue eyes way down south.

While I appear to be quite possibly a man without any country at all, Argentina is reconsidering me for immigration on the grounds that my tango partner in that film about the submarine captain is now the mother of twin boys with blond hair. She claims that I am the father and owe her a large sum of money from my film career royalties, so now at least Argentine lawyers are pressing for my immigration acceptance on the grounds that I owe and can pay lavish child support payments.

I currently reside in Costa Rica, because my skiing girlfriend from Aspen, Karen Smith, has rented me her hacienda here, but when she visits, I am to pitch my tent elsewhere. This reminds me of my younger years in Barranquilla, where I first felt snow in the Sierras de Santa Maria. A cable car there took me to the 4,900-meter summit, where I tried my best to ski but actually just cartwheeled, ass over teakettle, finally giving up on the idea until I went with Arnold to Aspen in Colorado and skied with Fritz Segenthaler and Klaus Obermeyer.

I admit that I have been fortunate to be so successful, and I confess that I have felt as though angels in heaven have guarded me throughout my entire voyage. My grandmothers both believed in the existence of angels, though both grandfathers and my own father had extreme doubts. I myself have always believed that Mary, Mother of Our Lord, must have been chosen but did ascend to heaven as an angel and might have been angelic, as possibly was Elizabeth, mother of John the Baptist, who was beheaded at Jezebel's desire.

In my bicycle-taxi days in Portal del Sur, Bolivar City, a suburb of Bogota, I had many near misses, with overloaded trucks and buses veering into my lane of the highway, only to be redirected as if by some hidden angels of mercy, perhaps beyond a distant cloud playing on their harps the benevolent music of tranquility at some frequency beyond what human ears can hear, possibly heard only by holy seers in their deepest of sleep attaining visions of the hereafter. Arnold, Klaus, Fritz, and even Karen agree, though I most deeply regret that I have not seen them now in so many years. I still write a letter or two and receive various emails from other celebrities whom I have met as well.

I feel most fortunate to have risen out of the depths of humanity in such squalor as poorest Bogota, but I appreciate that my ancestors were probably Plantagenet Europeans of the other, richer Bogota, for the Plantagenet royal blood of kings cannot be denied its inheritance indefinitely. Democracy, although popular, is short-lived in the span of history and might not survive the human race, and so it is possible that we shall see another, greater king upon the earth—another child, who shall dream the same as I, but who shall indeed become the real king for whom we patiently hope, going forth to conquer the hearts and souls of all mankind to deliver justice and create lasting peace.

It is only through the grace of God that we are clothed and fed each day of our lives. Without the angels who surround and guide our street crossings daily, we would be lost, imprisoned, or assassinated by fate and the darkness of ignorance. Grace be to God.

ABANDONED

RECALL SUFFERING FROM THE FLU AND VOMITING, WITH ALMOST NO heat supply in my house other than wood, which I had not gathered in sufficiency. I felt very sick, and with a fever of over one hundred, I checked into the only pet-friendly motel in South Fork, Colorado, with my main dog JP (the father of all my other dogs) and a very sick puppy that I no longer wanted to see suffer in the cold, because he was terminally ill. However, I had to leave JP's sister Sara, of whom I was most fond because she was a darling, at my freezing-cold, uninsulated house in Alpine Village, a remote subdivision on the outskirts of town going toward Del Norte. Sara had just delivered a litter of puppies in my Ford F150 pickup, and I had just given them each a half booster of puppy parvo virus and distemper vaccine. So I left poor Sara at the house with a very large bag of dog food, noticing her look of disapproval but promising her that I would return next dawn, and left for the motel in a heavy snowstorm while she busily breast-fed the entire litter.

Unfortunately my fever became steadily worse through the night, and I was too sick to even go for coffee the next morning, and my sick one-year-old, Houdini, did not pass the night well either. The wind picked up and howled, and the snowstorm became a blizzard. I prayed for the safety of my dog pack, but to no avail.

A nosey female neighbor with a drug addiction problem in her past and symptoms of bipolar disorder, who had handed out towels at the Glenwood Springs swimming pool and received snorts of cocaine as a tip—well, she had befriended the local veterinarian in Del Norte. She noticed my dogs at my house across the street, so she snooped on over and saw that their water dish had frozen, which constituted animal cruelty of some kind in her mind, so she gathered all the puppies and Sara and took them to her friend, the veterinarian. I never again saw Sara or those pups, who were all taken to City Market in Alamosa the next day and given away in the parking lot at the veterinarian's suggestion.

Life being cruel—and even more so in the high, remote Rocky Mountains, my one-year-old, Houdini, barked at a Mexican who had backed up into my car at a different motel in Monte Vista a whole month later. My poor little dog had lay there with no breath at all, on a warm blanket, with the rare fungus lung disease he had contracted from water that drips from the leaves of deciduous trees in Alabama or Louisiana. Somehow that fungus had spread to New Hampshire because of global warming the previous summer. Of course, the sheriff in Twin Mountain had decided that my five dogs constituted a threat to my blond-haired female neighbor with very big teats, for whom he had the hots. So me and my dogs felt very unwelcome because of his constant visits; he was just another bad cop who took bribes and was looking for one from me, so we left town instead.

Some flying saucers moving around strangely in the sky overhead, which I hadn't noticed but the dogs had begun barking at, seemed to be trying to warn the dogs of imminent danger—being the state police and a Sergeant Koler, who had become New Hampshire's leading expert on psychoanalysis, or so he claimed on routine traffic stops. My F150 Ford got impounded by him and towed off to his brother's garage. Nepotism, is it called?

All the dogs and I headed out west, but Macayla decided to run away in the Walmart parking lot in Canon City when we arrived in Colorado. I guess she got tired of so many endless hours of driving across country. Perhaps it's true that I was not the best dog owner, as I was suffering from undiagnosed slow thyroid.

My ex-wife's doctor recommended that I start radiation treatments for thyroid cancer. I left both her and that doctor in Avon, thinking maybe they were in cahoots.

Life is so cruel. Spotted Scotty got separated from the pack in Missouri, and Oscar Mayer failed to clear a barbed-wire fence in South

Fork while chasing his father, JP, who had been chasing something. Small children found Oscar tangled in barbed wire, and their father took him to the veterinarian, who recommended he be put down, because his leg couldn't be saved. But I had sold a parcel of land and had money for the operation, so Oscar became a three-legged dog, only to disappear in Illinois a year later.

Now this brings me back to life being cruel. I heard from Dusty Fullinwider, the real estate lady, that a dog loose in Alpine Village looked like one of my breed. Sara and JP had come from a litter owned by my neighbor Everett. Now Everett was missing all his toes, because when he had been falling-down drunk, his feet had frozen, and his gangrenous, green toes had been amputated to save his life. Everett had even put drugs in my coffee at his house in the hope of raping me, but he admitted the next day when I woke up that I had been too tough and uncooperative with his efforts, so I was not his type after all. Nice neighbor!

So anyway, I drove my F150 and JP to the far reaches of Alpine Slopes, number seven subdivision, and there running skittish between some abandoned summer cabins was a familiar-looking dog, definitely a son of JP. The crazy bitch neighbor of mine on cocaine had missed a puppy, which had gone wild and survived on that big bag of dog food that I had left behind, and now it was a year old perhaps. I coaxed it over to the truck with bits of food, then took it for a ride, but it growled and then fought with JP. It had become a wild, ravenous wolf, so I had to let it out of the truck. I never saw it again, but I was reassured that some unknown neighbor was still feeding it.

Eventually I was taken in an ambulance to some hospital with barred windows, where two young genius doctors agreed I had a failed thyroid and just needed to take a small pill daily. I got my dog JP back and my life improved steadily, even though JP got old and died. It was heartbreaking; he and his family and I had been through so much together. Now finally I had lost them all, but my godson, who had moved in with me, found a couple of rottweiler pups at McDonald's. It turned out their mother had bitten the mailman in Dalton, New Hampshire, and so the town sheriff there had gone over and sentenced her to the firing squad.

I was adopted by rich folks when just a baby, and they told me my racial ethnicity was starving Armenian. Then they fought, divorced, and separated. She went to an asylum, and I went ski racing up on high mountainsides to escape life's constant cruelty. So at a ski race long ago, when a blond chubby woman with a lot of mascara approached me and said she was my mother, I thought perhaps she was playing a practical joke on me. I jumped on the ski lift, went back up the mountainside, and never saw my birth mother again. How tragic.

I guess I was like that one wild dog abandoned in that blizzard, running free and by then such a wolf that there would be no further effort at domestication. And my birth mother was like the driver of a Ford F150 pickup truck. She had been sick with morning sickness and quarreling with her husband, my birth father, down there in Alabama, until finally she ran back to her aunt Doris, who was also a beauty, living there with her grandparents, the Hortons, in Brockton, Massachusetts.

Now I have to apologize to my uncle Charles, her brother, whom I expect to meet tomorrow at my race at Okemo Mountain Resort in Vermont. I have raced there since 1961, and I'm now seventy years old; he's seventy-six, being the youngest by far of his siblings.

Life is quite a tragedy unfolding, and I'm not fully aware yet why we must suffer so, and or why dogs, the most loving and obedient creatures, must suffer with us. Surely they don't deserve it. I think I won so many medals skiing in my long career just to distract me from life's unpleasantries and disappointments. The young lady whom I loved the most, when I was a young ski champion, died before her time of brain cancer. We had been separated by parents, destiny, and school, and she tried to call me one last time, but I didn't have a phone.

My own mother must have thought I was like a rabid dog or a wild sled dog gone to live in *The Call of the Wild*. I did. I'm still up there on that high mountain. Maybe we'll all be there across that great chasm, that great stream, when we die. We shall cross to the other side and see the ones we miss so dearly, taken from us by this cruel world, but then we shall reunite and be together again. I hope so. I sure miss you all! Amen.

STREET FIGHTER

WAS HUNGRY IN THE STREETS OF NEW YORK. TOO PREOCCUPIED with his new wife, my father had kicked me out of the house for the Oedipus complex. He said I could live in an abandoned room on top of 464 Park Avenue, and that the doorman would still let me in, but there were a lot of spiderwebs and flies. At sixteen years old, I enlisted in a good private school downtown, and the very strict teacher decided we should do some creative writing.

"I am living on top of a building in New York City, a hateful place full of noise and traffic and all-night sirens. I have no heat but manage to sleep and dream that I am falling through the air upside down while staring through the windows at myself in doors." Yes, I had suicidal tendencies.

The police were looking for me on Fifth Avenue because I had walked out of too many restaurants without paying the breakfast bill. "Hey, there's that kid. Call the police." Whistles blowing and me running.

So there's this friendly African American shining shoes and making small change, enough to survive. I tell him that I'm a starving kid living on the streets and that I need a job, so maybe I can help him shine shoes. So he calls over two guys in brand new suits with hats and says, "Shine their shoes, kid."

I get busy shining away. Buff, polish, spit on their shoes too? What? "Okay, where's my pay?" They drop some dollars on the pavement and I bend over to pick them up. They begin kicking the shit out of me with those damn pointed shoes of theirs.

"What are you doing that for?" I'm bewildered. They're Italian. Maybe I was in Little Italy on the edge of their borough? They gave me my new job indeed: street fighter.

My friend in New Hampshire, Ernie Cavallaro, arrived there to hide out in a cabin with a gun. He told me, "When I sleep, my wife watches the door with my loaded pistol. Yes, I had that same education in New York!"

It paid off when I moved to Silverton, Colorado, where every miner wanted to test me because I wasn't one. Every Friday night and Saturday, another brawl after beer. Luckily they were all drunk, and I knew to not finish my beer. One of them had been a boxer at Fort Lewis College, in Durango, but I kept him away with jabs and managed to stay on my feet, because if you were to fall, then you would get that New York treatment. I had a good memory of life in New York, though I lived there only a few months and knew enough to leave for greener pastures.

(Obviously that big shot Donald T. never got this New York education, or he would shut the f**k up and not run his motormouth into so much trouble.)

REBEL RYAN

BOB BEATTIE DIDN'T NEED ANY OTHER EXCUSE TO BAR ME FROM the team. I had been placed under the tutelage of Rebel Harry Ryan, whose mother had been born in South Carolina, and Beattie already knew that my biological father was from Alabama, although Louis had told me that my father was from Los Angeles and my origins were from the Caucasus.

I was a confused nineteen-year-old, which is an understatement. I now lived in Boulder, Colorado, where I had just been accepted by the University of Colorado (CU), but my father refused to pay the necessary tuition. So I was basically just a ski bum with some connection to the US ski team, and the men's coach, Gordi Eaton, had let me crash in his apartment a few nights when it was decided that Harry Rebel Ryan would be my compadre.

Rebel taught me to drive cars, so I did gain some valuable instruction from him. In later years, under the influence of various hippie drugs, I finally managed to drive my Ford Thunderbird at 130 mph without crashing it, and I have only Harry Rebel Ryan to thank for his diligent instruction.

He found us a place to live with two of the nicest people on earth, young ladies enrolled at CU and studying to become lawyers—Virginia "Swifty" Swift, his girlfriend, also known as Ginny, and her roommate, who at first was less enthusiastic. Anne Stewart, from Baltimore, was an avid lifelong equestrian who, had I been fourteen years older, would have made an excellent wife. I didn't need to propose, however, as there were only two beds in the house and Anne liked to sleep with almost no clothing. We both awoke just as we were doing something of a subconscious, primitive nature. OMG. Quickly we refrained and went back to sleep, but I had grievous feelings of guilt, though we continued to dwell in the same bed.

I drove Anne's car. Then Harry drove her car and crashed it into a semi-truck near Arapahoe Basin, and I hitchhiked off, thinking it would be easier for the three of them to get a ride, which they did—also with a semi-truck. Anne never forgave me, thinking I had abandoned her in her time of need, and somehow the crash was my fault, because going skiing had been my idea when they actually had needed to study for term exams.

I thought Rebel Harry was my friend, but Beattie had hinted to him that only one of us would be on the Olympic team, so Harry saw his moment of opportunity and slowly turned on me, trying to confuse my madness by adding to it in every possible way to ensure his position, which he soon fulfilled. As a member of the 1968 Olympic Team, he would need to pay Beattie $12,500, which his parents didn't have. Neither did my grandmother, though I asked her at the bequest of Gordi Eaton. We had probably both thought the Olympics were free for the well-deserved champions, only to be disappointed by Beattie, who had hotels in Lake Placid that probably needed renovation.

So Harry, a brilliant CU student whose parents did pay his tuition, received a suitcase from the chemistry lab, possibly containing ingredients for the African community, that he was to deliver to East Colfax in Denver. Then the police approached him, for he had been set up as well, and that was the end of his ski career. He was released on probation and prohibited from leaving Rutland, Vermont, for the next five years. He became a lawyer there, hitting the books and making his parents happy—and therefore himself also.

(Thanks so much to Harry "Rebel" Ryan, who taught me how to drive a car so that I lived until old age.)

DIANNE

THE FIRST TIME I BEHELD YOUR FACE, YOU THOUGHT I HAD PERHAPS been lost in space but now was found upon the earth. You smiled and said, with mirth, "Where the hell did you drop in from?"

I immediately thought you were a hippie who might be on drugs. But no, you were just being sarcastic, witty, struggling, middle-class you from Loraine, Ohio, where the Puerto Ricans were buying all the houses on your block and thus eroding your parents' golden goose egg of retirement, their home, which was just about all they would ever own. But then your mother had grown ill and died—you told me she had passed away the previous year—so you became a freshman flunking out of Ohio State who'd just as soon leave and go to Colorado or any adventure anywhere. You climbed into my car with your boyfriend, "Sandblast" Ken Safranski, and we accelerated down the treed lane of Puerto Rican houses and onto the big road on the shore of Lake Ontario, headed toward the interstate highway.

We camped in a dark blue spruce forest on a Rocky Mountain pass, and in the night you awoke as the frost was gleaming on our sleeping bags, and we talked a few sentences, but soon we were hugging each other just to stay warm and there was another kind of radiance. We felt a fatal attraction, and I marveled at the sparkle in your eyes, which was the same as the thousands of stars at our high altitude where the air is less dense, and we had arrived at the edge of vast space, looking up at a rising crescent moon, with a coyote howling of loneliness on a distant mountainside. Perhaps it had lost its mate, but we had definitely discovered each other, and not being sure where our great adventure would lead us, our hearts leaped for joy, as they had never traveled this road into these deep feelings.

There was no going back, and every second—every breath—was just one more exciting adventure. Your teeth were so white, and your eyes were the brightest stars in my new heaven.

We built a cabin on a high mountainside, and there were no other houses within seven miles. We were at the tree line, but winter was coming, and ten feet of snow would drift over and cover our seventeen-foot-high cabin. It became necessary to vacate our high mountain home for five months, leaving in the first snows of November and returning in early May, when we would climb back up on our skis on the patches of snow, as flowers began rushing out of the newly exposed earth into full bloom everywhere. The brilliance of the warm, high summer sun was us. I lay beside you as you slept and thought what a great miracle this had become—you nestled in my arms, the full moon above the peaks.

And then one spring a few years later, you decided, after reading the stories of your new close friend Janice, to go off to Europe to Avoca, a place by the sea in Ireland where she had been. I never saw you again, although I received half a dozen letters; you said you were married and had two children, both boys. Then your husband cheated on you and left, and you were coming to America again to attend a funeral, and would I pick you up at JFK Airport on Long Island?

But I lost the piece of paper with the flight number and the time of arrival, two hundred miles south of my bleak, meager existence picking rocks behind a road grader for three dollars an hour. And I never saw you again ...

CRAIG MILLAR

C RAIG MILLAR, MY HIGH SCHOOL COMPANION IF NOT FRIEND, HAD gone off to Vietnam, a country full of insects, sand, and monsoons, to fight the enemy in a war that President John Fitzgerald Kennedy had tried to avoid, and we found out much later that this war had caused JFK's assassination. Big corporations, including the military industrial establishment, were gung ho for war, because war makes money for the privileged few but headaches for society as a whole. Rumor had it that Craig, being popular, young, and friendly, was picked to drive a truck somewhere from the DMZ on the day it was overrun by thirty thousand North Vietnamese regulars who had just entered the war in a full-scale invasion. After a lot of napalm was dropped, the Third Marine Division and Craig recaptured their original positions, at least temporarily, to make our president in the White House, Lyndon Baines Johnson, a happy man lighting a cigar.

After his tour of duty, Craig decided not to reenlist, and his proud father, the ski patrol director at Cannon Mountain Ski Resort, gave him a good recommendation to be hired at Santa Fe Ski Basin in New Mexico, and he moved there with his eighteen-year-old girlfriend, Tracey Pierce, not far behind.

That's about when I made the scene on the New Mexico Pro Ski Tour. I finished third place as the young eighteen-year-old Marlin Ross from Utah was the slalom superstar that season. My only victory came weeks later, when at Apache Basin I won because Marlin, in the second run of the finals, refused to switch courses, and so the start official disqualified him for too much LSD ... or so Marlin later admitted.

Meanwhile in Santa Fe Basin, my future wife, being perhaps sixteen years old then, was skiing the sidelines, watching the race, and wondering what foreign country had sent me as its ambassador, the answer being New England—Vermont, New Hampshire, and so on. Perhaps our eyes met, as she was a radiant and attractive beauty, the daughter of the ski school director Carl Severe, a teammate of Stein Erikson on the 1952 Norwegian Olympic Team.

Mynx was coming to town, and after the race, we all met up and decided to drink far too much beer, pitchers upon pitchers, because the name of the owner of the ski area was Kingsbury Pitcher, according to Craig, who had many wild stories.

Tracey was quite a catch, with her fine voluptuous figure (her mother was half Spanish!), wild tantalizing eyes, and wide smile. She had never been traumatized like the rest of us. Mynx was excited about her too, and they ran off somewhere, but the car broke down, so they camped out, huddling together near a fire.

I met Tracey's parents that summer in Vermont, as she had broken up with Craig and was then dating Brian Pendleton. Her father wanted me to use my chain saw to cut down several hundred trees for him. Being not too bright and wishing to escape Tracey's mother's glare, I ran off into the woods to burn a lot of chain-saw oil, make smoke, and—I hoped—get paid for it.

Brian, being sort of allergic to work, stayed at the house to converse with the mother, charm her, and be the gentleman his father had hoped he might become. Tracey's father, Cedric, was a prominent teacher of history at nearby Lyndon State College.

Anyone marrying Tracey would have received the equivalent of a full scholarship plus two hundred and fifty acres. Tracey, however, liked rock concerts, loud music, drug dealers, and musicians, and Brian and I didn't quite fit the bill. And besides, her mother really didn't want me on the property. Oh well, at least I got paid—and I had one hot date with Tracey, who looked even better with her clothes off.

Because Santa Fe wouldn't rehire him, Craig then transferred to Burke Mountain, where he would become the new patrol director and hire Brian, who would bite off the ear of mountain manager Ford

Hubbard in a drunken brawl at the Bear Den. Amazingly they didn't fire Brian, as Ford's ear was sewed back on at the hospital. However, Brian wasn't rehired the following winter. As for Tracey, she moved to Arkansas to grow strawberries, as her mother had taught her, and avoid me and Brian.

RACER ROB

MET MY FRIEND ROB IN TELLURIDE, THOUGH ORIGINALLY HE WAS FROM Connecticut, a few towns over from where I had once lived. He became a painter, as dyslexia prohibited him from attending college. Oh well, college is not entirely necessary for earning a living, but the cliques of elite formed there last a lifetime. For instance, my Mynx, who attended Middlebury College, looked further and further down on me for the rest of our lives, especially after she married a multimillionaire who, of course, was deeply impressed by her Middlebury credentials.

I never graduated from college myself, as my father, who decided I was a bad investment and would never fit into any elitist clique, abandoned any commitment to such an endeavor. So I, like Rob, fit into that cast of characters in the blue collar—not white collar—world. I tried being a ski instructor for a while, but I managed to get fired by all seven ski schools within six years, which in Telluride was a record.

Rob continued painting but managed to meet the daughter of my client, her father, an avid skier from Pennsylvania. They married within a few months and produced a child who was amazingly unlike Rob, especially after the divorce. That child played piano at Carnegie Hall in New York at the age of twelve.

So twenty years later, Rob and I were still skiing, and it was opening week in November at Keystone in Colorado, where a few thousand Denverites—half of them snowboarders—had congregated, like followers of an unheralded ski god, to celebrate their religion of medical marijuana and mayhem, a display of wild pandemonium upon the mountain of joy!

The first day out, on his last run of the day, at about one o'clock in the afternoon, as we were tiring from being out of shape, Rob decided to pass me at the bottom, as he likes to display his skiing skills. Suddenly a snowboarder in front of him fell, with the snowboard slanting in Rob's direction, and the collision was unavoidable. So Rob went to Frisco hospital, where a day later his shoulder was pinned.

Meanwhile I continued to ski each day and lunch at Spoon's Café, closest to the lifts at the main Riverside base, a maze of pseudo-European, five-story hotels with shops, restaurants, and restrooms.

The guy sitting next to me seemed friendly, so I begin talking with him about the ice, accidents, and reckless snowboarders, and then I told him that I had once been a ski instructor in Telluride, where I had taught two children, nine-year-old Peyton Manning and seven-year-old Eli Manning, who was more athletically gifted but far less analytical than Peyton. Of course the guy had heard of them, because they had both won Super Bowls as starring quarterbacks of their respective teams, the Indianapolis Colts and the New York Giants. It turned out this fellow, Chris Condit, knew them and especially their father, Archie Manning, who had been quarterback of the New Orleans Saints.

Peyton and Eli's mother was a tall blond track star from maybe Texas A&M, and their uncle was tall like their mother, also blond, from Phoenix. "Damn," I protested, "they could both have been Olympic-caliber skiers on the US Ski Team. Peyton, who was nine, told me, 'Our father says skiing is a nowhere sport and we're both going to be football quarterbacks.' They knew what they were going to be at very young ages. Amazing, they could have been—"

"Well, they were. They were indeed," Chris Condit corrected me.

"Well, if you see them, tell them that you met their old ski instructor and that he says there is still time for them to be ski racers!" I laughed.

Maybe the joke was on me, but the far worse joke was on poor Rob. Having left the hospital, he arrived back at the motel in a taxi, claiming that his surgeon had been from the Steadman Clinic in Vail. "Maybe it was the same doctor who operated yesterday on Julia Mancuso, the awesome Olympic gold medalist from California," he said. It turned out to have been a different doctor, though from the same clinic.

In the ensuing days of early-season skiing, as I counted seventeen toboggans going down the mountain, I said my prayers to Jesus: "Oh please, Lord, keep me in thy grace. Have mercy upon us." Snowboarders were falling in front of me and behind me, and twenty of them with ten skiers all within a foot of each other looked like an interstate highway pileup in the making.

Rob will be able to ski in another eight weeks. Thank you, Lord!

PARALLEL UNIVERSE

Though I am not the king and I only reside
in the temple of my one body,
The Lord instructs me daily not to turn backward
while on the road to His Salvation.
I hear different parables, and I compose different psalms of praise.
Could there be Christ the Redeemer in a different universe?
I am a sinner, Lord. Why me? Why do you love me?
How can you love me from so far, even a different universe?
I am only your pen and not your mind!
I write down everything you tell me respectfully,
Because you are my right arm, which is my
Salvation, and my left arm, which is Mercy.
You are my shield and protector, and my waistband is the Truth.
In your church today, each member spoke, but I had nothing to say.
You are only at my fingertips and cannot reach my tongue.
Even so, I am glad at this written gift you
made of me, a testimony of Truth.
Thus I thank you for everything I have, which
may in others' minds be very little.
What I have been given is sufficient for me;
I ask for no more than what I have,
Because if I had more, it would be too much and
I would spend all my time giving it away.
Where can I tell them that these gifts have
come from other than you, Lord?

I have achieved nothing on my own, only through my
earthly father and you, my more distant heavenly father,
Though you may be dearer to my heart, because your love is true
If we just ask for it and receive you in our hearts.
Please enter the temple of my body and
dwell there for my health's sake,
Because without you, I will die in despair. I will proclaim
that I am great and this would be an illusion.
I would only fall from greatness and my big tower; you
alone are my high tower and defense, forever.

ST. CHARLIE MUNROW

DUNCAN MILLAR, BEING YOUNG AND VIBRANT WITH MOOD SWINGS, needs other people in his life and so attaches himself to a wide variety of riffraff whom he finds mostly in front of the library in Littleton, on the sidewalk near Porfidos where they buy cigarettes and, if opportunity presents itself, pills from each other, this being America, the world's pharmacy. There must be trillions at stake in the global market.

And since, of course, the American military has made gains in Afghanistan into the poppy fields, now everyone who can't afford OxyContin can at least now purchase the half-price alternative, heroin.

So where in all creation did Duncan Millar find this latest chum from Lancaster named Charlie Munrow? At the first ski race to which we took him, he managed to steal Brian Pendleton's ski poles from the base lodge. Then he veered out of his line to physically contact Duncan Millar going forty miles an hour into the finish line, but not to arrive …

"Ha ha," laughed Charlie Monrow, skiing up to the base lodge, where Brian was fuming still over his lost poles.

"Oh, you have my poles!" screamed Brian the Bear Pendleton at Charlie Munrow.

I wish Duncan Millar would redeposit some of these people, maybe take them back where he found them or at least take them up on Sugar Hill to Paul Hayward, who has a crew of such people to whom he feeds racks of beer—cases and kegs—on a daily basis.

Up there is Longjohn, Carter, and Crazy Joe. You name them, they're all there picking fiddleheads for Paul, then logging, then raking, then roofing for Carter, who actually has a brain but was shipped up from Fall River after being suspected of several bank robberies, which were never solved. No truth to it at all.

So Charlie Munrow entertained us by jumping off the railroad trestle over the Connecticut River, where the sign reads, "No jumping. Trespassing here is a criminal offense." Charlie was a good logger. If nothing else, he would simply snap trees off by their roots barehanded, no chain saw needed. That indeed was green, saving gas.

Charlie was also a genius at fixing things such as bicycles and four-wheeler-quadro-whatevers, then racing them helmetless on snowmobile trails while drinking from a beer can or twelve. Of course, he had long ago lost his driver's license because of excess consumption of alcohol, which now posed a problem, with several law enforcement officers in Littleton giving chase and catching him.

No problem. Charlie merely beat them all up and escaped to downtown on Veterans' Bridge. With the January temperatures well below zero and officers closing in from both ends of the bridge, he did what any normal person would do. He jumped off the bridge, hit the ice forty feet below, and then swam half a mile in the twenty-eight-degree water. No problem.

No problem for the police either, as they caught him and pulled him naked from the river. Oh well, a few more months in Woodsville Correctional Facility, which we call "the farm."

So Charlie Munrow got out at long last and—wonderful joy!—came back up to our house looking for his buddy, Duncan Millar, who was busy with a cell phone stuck in his ear, as usual. Being a genius, Charlie went into Millar's room and borrowed his hooded sweatshirt, sunglasses, and blue jeans, then proceeded to the garage and borrowed my ten-speed bicycle bought in a yard sale somewhere.

Charlie pedaled on down to the Irving Gasamat, about two hundred yards away under the interstate underpass, where he pulled a knife on the new employee. The eighteen-year-old kid of Asian descent from some distant place had ventured out into the world, on his first experience away from home, and whom did he meet? Charlie Munrow, with a butcher knife, who wanted not only the cash register change and bills, but also a variety of sexual pleasures, this being past midnight and no one in the store.

The latest additions to our house, visiting on a daily basis, are Kevin, who had an elevator fall on his head causing a personality change, and Irish Dave, who might be from Boston but wants to mow our lawn three times a week and get paid for it. "But Dave, the grass hasn't even grown yet. It's still winter!"

Paul Hayward hasn't been doing so well since his house was condemned up there on the crest of Sugar Hill. Yes, they tore it down, so now we call him the Big Boss of Nothing! Longjohn, who dried out and quit smoking, will soon be released from the halfway house. Carter is still at large somewhere doing a large roof, maybe the Penn. And Kevin has missed softball all summer after going snowboarding with me last winter and refusing to go up the lift. His feet have grown since he had used the lift as a kid, and now his toes hang over the edge of the snowboard.

"Mine do too, Kevin."

"It just doesn't feel right." So he skipped his return to snowboarding, but then he showed up out of the clear blue sky, so I told him to go live in my abandoned trailer in Wells River.

Chad, a cousin of Crazy Joe—at least a spiritual cousin, as he has the same ailment—has stopped by in his car. At least he can drive and has no criminal record. Duncan Millar and his bride need a ride to the hospital, because she is expecting—I would imagine—today?

So soon another life will come into our midst. Hmm ...

It is my sincere hope that the newborn baby will be utterly loved and achieve great success in this world of entanglements. A new member for the team, too, I suspect, because we need one—perhaps a normal one, but then what is normal anyway?

ELI AND PEYTON

DESCENDED FROM VIKING RAIDERS OF NORMANDY, THE NELSONS were most likely second-class citizens in England, as were most immigrants. So they packed their bags and came to Arundel, Maryland, all four generations probably on the same boat in 1679. Their descendent Ambrose Nelson II fought in the Revolutionary War, and his grandchild Henry was born in South Carolina and died in Tennessee. Henry's great-granddaughter would be the mother of New Orleans Saints quarterback Archie Manning.

I had never heard of him when Fred Libby asked, "Don't you know who Archie Manning is?" I didn't watch a lot of football on television, as I had left home at sixteen and dealt more with homelessness and finding my next meal than football. The New Orleans Saints had been the farthest thing from my mind.

Until a tall blond woman and a tall blond man, who I assumed to be her husband but was in fact her brother, brought two children, ages seven and nine, into the ski school meeting room and introduced them to me. I informed them that I would be teaching them to ski all week and asked if they had ever. Yes, they had once or twice.

So out the door we went and put on our skis, there at Gorrono Park in Telluride, in the pre-Christmas world of white frozen splendor. I determined that they were good skiers—not highly motivated, but extremely well coordinated. They did everything I told them, so in just five days we were skiing slalom on Apex Glade, the hardest run on the mountain, covered in deep moguls and ruts between trees on a forty-five-degree pitch.

"You two boys are excellent skiers and could be Olympic material," I explained to them.

"Our father says skiing is a bad sport, and we're going to be football players!" they informed me.

I would drop them off at four o'clock every afternoon, where their tall, athletic-looking mother was waiting for them like a cheerleader. I had no idea she had been an NCAA track star for Texas A&M. I still hadn't met Archie, but I finally did on their last day with me. The boys, Peyton and Eli, probably told him I had been like an Austrian drill sergeant, so I can't remember too well, but maybe I got a forty-dollar tip, nothing too grand. Peyton had been analytical, asking all kinds of questions about why I skied and how much I got paid on the US ski team, whereas Eli was more the mimicker. I would show him what to do and he would follow behind me, imitating my every move and then laughing about it all.

The joke, of course, was on me when I became aware of their brilliant football careers as quarterbacks in the Super Bowl, which Eli won twice and Peyton once. Archie, short and squat, had probably not been the best running quarterback who ever lived. Perhaps he had realized that his boys would have a better future with that gazelle track star as their mother. Archie and fast Fred Libby were sort of from the same vein: terrific ambition and a keen, quick-witted sense that life is short, so they should make every play a touchdown, because there is no second chance.

"That's the way I ski," I explained to those boys. "You gotta go for it, give it your best, ski your best, and be the fastest. We're here to win!"

But I never did get any Super Bowl tickets.

GERRY KNAPP, A.K.A. "THE KNAPPER"

WAS STILL A CHILD AT BROMLEY MOUNTAIN IN VERMONT WHEN MY father, struggling with his stem christies, and I in my snowplow schuss going straight down encountered a bamboo slalom course set for the Rice father and two sons. They all wore those old slalom hats with earflaps and visors, like baseball hats but made of leather, not cotton. The slalom poles had little blue, red, and yellow flags attached and it looked like fun, so I skied by a few of them in imitation, but I was soon yelled at to stay off their course. It was a wake-up call that skiing was for the rich and Anglo-Saxon, my father told me, adding that Austrians were by far the best skiers on this planet.

At prep school, I felt some of that same prejudice when issued my first jumping skis, the bear-trap bindings of which were mounted two inches behind center on my pair. No one took notice for three dismal weeks, during which my ski tips dropped upon takeoff and I landed and cartwheeled on the knoll. My ski jumping career was not looking promising, as I was immensely discouraged and soaking wet with my clothes full of snow from back-to-back crashes.

My roommate that first year at Holderness was a Pakistani who prayed early every morning to Mecca, a faraway place where Allah was God. Eventually I would teach him to fight our English teacher, Fleck, from Bowdoin College in Maine, where just white people went to school.

The winners of the Eastern Junior Championships were all Anglo-Saxon, Irish, or French-Canadian American. Skiing was the last great white hope, with blond Penny Pitou from Gunstock, New Hampshire, winning silver medals in the Squaw Valley Olympics. White people everywhere had money and sportscars and went skiing on weekends. Nonwhite people lived in ghettos, and their children played basketball and track. Just a few were inducted into baseball, where Mickey Mantle was my favorite until Hank Aaron hit that ninth-inning home run to beat the New York Yankees. Hank Aaron was as dark as night itself. Then the So-Jo kid, Willie Mays, ran deep into the box in center field and caught a deep fly ball hit over his head, that no white person had ever attempted to catch in that fashion, and the Giants won the World Series.

There were some tough, mean boxers who were also African American, but nobody dared say anything about racism in sports until Cassius Clay changed his name to Muhammad Ali. I never should have listened to him, as identifying with those poor underdogs gave me some strength but led me into an identity crisis with my Anglo-Saxon teammates on the US Ski Team, who presumed I was neither Catholic nor pure white. It was my young, undeveloped, immature brain that detested them, like the Rice brothers who had yelled at me to stay off their Anglo-Saxon slalom course.

I wanted to ski and win slalom races, because deep down inside me was a fighter, and losing was not in my nature.

"Hi, I'm Gerry. Get in the car!" said Gerry Knapp, who was also a ski racer. He was from Stowe, at least temporarily, because his sister had moved there and married a mob boss.

"Really?" I was naive. *Why would a mob boss live in Stowe?* I wondered, having seen them mostly on television or theater newsreels.

Gerry Knapp was four years older than me, but he was from a wise race—Jewish Yugoslav and some Saxon back there somewhere, for the Knapps were Austrian. So we had a lot in common, racing against the Anglo-Saxon rich kids, many of whom were raised with a Saxon work ethic and soon dropped out of the sport to take jobs, marry, and raise children. Not us ski bums, for we were enjoying the sport too much.

Gerry said, "Take a hit of this reefer." I did, but it wasn't my first.

Rebel Ryan had passed me my first joint in Boulder, Colorado, two years earlier when we dragged a thirty-foot-wide Christmas tree into the house through several doorways, until it became stuck and the doors wouldn't close.

"How much money did you bring with you?" Gerry asked me, somewhere near Indiana on our drive out west to go race Aspen and Steamboat in the national races called the Wild West Classic, Bear Valley in California, Jackson Hole in Wyoming, Steamboat in Colorado, and so forth.

"Well, I have twenty-two cans of kippered snacks in tin cans and ... Whoops, only seven dollars!" We were indeed the poor kids en route to race the rich white kids.

"Oh my God," said Gerry, and mused for a while before stopping for gas and coffee.

"I'm not going to kick you out of my car here in the middle of nowhere," he finally replied. "Do you have some friends out west where we can stay when we get to Aspen?"

"Well, my friend John Stirling has a place near Carbondale on Missouri Heights ... and I have a girlfriend who's going to school in Steamboat, if we get there, named Wendy Coughlin."

When we arrived in Steamboat, Wendy said on the phone to wait till after dark and use the hidden ladder to climb into her second-floor dorm window. She got expelled for that eventually, but said college didn't agree with her lifestyle anyway.

At the end of that long ski racing season, the Knapper showed up in North Conway and said, "Get in my car." I did. He then added that I owed him and that he had been instructed by his bosses to drive me to Stowe nonstop, because "they" wanted me *not* to race in the final race of the year, the Mount Washington American Inferno. I didn't try to jump out, because I had to go to Stowe and retrieve a Peugeot racing bicycle that had been delivered to my client but not paid for.

"Well, if you're down and out—with no money, no career, and no future—you can always join the family," said the man in Stowe from behind his thick glasses at the kitchen table.

The next morning at five o'clock, I found my way out of the house and somehow found that bicycle. Maybe someone had dropped it off for me. It was April 23, 1969, and twenty-six degrees with a dusting of snow on the road. I escaped en route to Plymouth, New Hampshire, 110 miles away, and got within twenty-five miles. Then my hands froze, so somebody made a telephone call, and John French came and picked me up, wondering just what in hell I was up to.

The next morning after a six-thirty breakfast, I began pedaling toward Meredith, New Hampshire, where—frozen again—I called Wendy Bryant, my landlord in North Conway, who sent Danny Del Rossi to pick up me and my bicycle on the highway in Chocorua, New Hampshire. It was two days before the Inferno Ski Race. My frozen hands would possibly have time to heal.

EVACUATION AT
PORTILLO 1965

I T'S ALWAYS A GOOD YEAR WHEN YOU'RE SEVENTEEN YEARS OLD, because your fresh new life is exciting, with each fresh new day full of adventure. It's good to be alive and have somewhere new to go and something new to see. When you're a child, every desert is a delight, and when you're a seventeen-year-old male, the girls have suddenly become young women with wavy hair and bright beaming eyes expecting adventure from you.

I had been in a lot of trouble as a sixteen-year-old, and I was unsure exactly what had caused such a messy year in my life. Would my own father forgive my trespasses and allow me to go back to Portillo, Chile?

My governess, Caroline, said wisely, "This is not a good week to ask your father if you may go to South America. He's in a bad mood because of the stock market. I'll let you know when he's in a good mood so that you'll get a positive result." Caroline found the optimum time for me to pop the question.

He frowned for about fifteen seconds, but then his frown went away and he asked, wanting to be sure that my request was genuine, "Did Caroline ask you to ask me about this? They have plans to go to England and see their relatives—if, of course, they won't be needed here to babysit you all summer."

I had been living with the French family all winter on skiing weekends and had competed and won at the US Junior National Ski

Championships, yet it had been decided that I should return to my father's house for the duration of the summer. My stepmother, Dorothy, who was far less enthusiastic about my return, had said to my father, "Darling, my children are now your dear children, and this extra one from your ill first wife is equally as ill. What can be done with him?"

My father said, "Yes, I'll arrange with my secretary, Mildred, to purchase an airline ticket for you for three weeks or—"

"Six weeks, please, Father!"

"Okay." He relented and smiled, because he knew this would be great news to my stepmother.

There was sibling rivalry at the French home, and my former friend, upon becoming my almost brother, had turned against me, and their daughter Janice wanted more time alone with her overworked mother, Hope. Plus my former home was no longer waiting for me with open arms. I boarded the Pan American Airways turboprop with stops in Miami, Panama, and Lima before it landed in Santiago, which means St. James—although that could hardly have concerned me at seventeen, as I was no angel in waiting.

Then the long, slow cog train from Los Andes to Portillo. While I had been waiting for it the previous year, the owner at my hotel had said, "There are really bad people looking for you. Go with my Syrian sons to the statue of Jesus. They won't be looking for you there." But that year had been mostly washed from my mind because of electric shock treatments. It was as though I had been born all over again at seventeen, minus a few recent years, so I was thinking more like a twelve-year-old.

The train climbed slowly through the barren Andean valley to Rio Blanco (White River), a tiny hamlet where children ran barefoot through just a few inches of freshly fallen snow. The Chilean peasants had nothing but rags to wear, but they wore huge smiles upon seeing the daily train, which in that smallest dot on the planet was like the *Queen Mary* entering New York harbor.

I piled my clothes and ski boots in the small closet of my bunk room in the Grand Hotel Portillo (little port) on the shores of Laguna Del Inca, where a princess fleeing from the Spanish Conquistadors had preferred to drown rather than be captured. Hundreds of years had passed since then, and now it became an opulent resort, a jewel in the Andes Mountains of Chile.

I had the Reese brothers for roommates, but one of them, Jerry, would be leaving for the Rotunda, a big circular rock house down by the ski lift that housed the ski patrol, of which he would become a member. Rig wanted to join the ski patrol too, but like me, he was considered too young. Of course, in 1965 there wasn't a whole lot to do in Portillo, which had one telephone—or maybe three, but they were linked by lines crossed by avalanches. Luckily I had brought my chess set with me, but now I needed to find someone who enjoyed the game, down in the hotel living room.

I was in luck, because a twenty-year-old Cornell University student named Ronald "Ron" Hock was playing chess against himself with a clock. I would never present any great challenge to him, beating him only once when he lost his queen. He knew every possible opening and defense: Sicilian Defense, Queen's Gambit, and so on. He often opened up knight pawn to K3, then diagonally in front of each rook or castle he would place his bishops in a crossfire at the center of the chessboard. I had never seen anything like it, although my father—and also Othmar Schneider, the ski school director—would sometimes play one bishop in such a manner, but rarely both.

Ron, from New York, was no great skier or athlete, but his parents must have felt compelled to send the city boy out into the world of adventure to become a man, get out of his mother's hair, and do more than just errands with the house servants all summer—especially since his parents must have had adventure plans of their own. So we played a lot of chess, every evening for almost two weeks.

A massive storm brewing somewhere in the Pacific was expected to hit central Chile and dump as much as five feet of snow on Portillo. Ron wanted to be on the ski patrol, like Jerry Reese, and he was waiting for his application to be reviewed by Henry Purcell, the owner, and Othmar Schneider, the director of everything on snow, including the ski school and ski patrol. Othmar had won the 1952 Olympic slalom, narrowly beating Stein Erikson, the Norwegian.

Othmar summoned me and said that my skiing was not improving and that I was wasting my time imitating Willy Bogner and Fritz

Wagnerberger, both German downhillers who did some strange counter-rotation windup before each turn, unlike the Austrians, who always faced downhill.

Then the good news came that Ron had been hired by the ski patrol. Beaming with excitement, he would be packing up his things to move to the rotunda.

The wind was blowing sixty miles per hour, and the ski lifts closed early because the chairs were almost swinging into the towers supporting the cables. It began to snow like hell, and the wind was almost deafening.

"This is a big, dangerous storm, and we're asking everyone to stay indoors for two days, possibly three, until the wind subsides," announced Othmar, with Henry Purcell standing behind him. The hotel's electric lights flickered and then went out, and candles and a few lanterns were lit. The snow was piling up, and someone said, "Over eight feet deep already!" Now there was no one with whom to play chess, and even the Chilean Army ski troops had retreated to their housing, a mile distant.

It was all gray outside with swirling snow, so I went to bed and slept a deep sleep until I heard someone yelling, "Help!" It was coming from outside, three stories below. I could hear window shutters banging open, possibly from Othmar and Uka's room not too far distant. (He had a Chilean mistress.)

Then there was banging on the metal doors below, and I could barely hear the loud cry, "*Avalancha!*" which is Chilean for avalanche. We sat up in our bunks, wondering what new excitement this storm had brought with it. I decided to get dressed and go downstairs. Men were handing out shovels, and I took one, and they said that yes, I would need my skis. It was now becoming visibly white outdoors, for night had ended. The near-naked man who had been yelling had crawled from the rotunda. It could have been Dick Hawkins or Jerry Reese.

I made my way to the lower side of the rotunda, where a soldier had opened a back door. As I looked up the staircase, it was full of snow and dripping water from broken pipes. I began shoveling upward, until finally someone pointed at me and said, "He's too young. Get him out of here." It was tall Victor of the ski school. I was exhausted by then anyway, so I left the stairwell and went back outside as a dozen Chilean soldiers came inside to replace me.

I climbed up the icy debris to the other side of the building, where the snow was thirty feet higher. An avalanche possibly forty feet deep in a valley had accumulated from a mile-wide scree field beneath two thousand feet of sheer cliffs, up against which the fierce, unyielding wind had piled a mile-wide snow drift, which had sheared off to cause this destruction. The stone house had withstood most of the blow, but the roof had been blown off by the two-hundred-mile-per-hour wind preceding the avalanche. The ski patrollers in the upper bunks were missing. Ron, the last hired, had been in an upper bunk; the lower bunks were cherished by the veteran patrollers.

I stood exhausted on the packed avalanche until I was ordered to leave the premises. Where I had stood, suddenly an arm popped up through the snow. They were all dug out, still alive but terribly cold, and loaded on toboggans, which carried them up to the hotel one by one. They all cried, almost in unison, "I don't want to die. I don't want to die!" But once inside, where their chilled bodies warmed, each person hemorrhaged and died. They had been crushed internally by the densely packed avalanche snow, which is much like solid ice.

I had lost a friend. Jerry Reese had been on a lower bunk, as had Dick Hawkins. At first, they thought this must be some kind of nightmare, but then they pushed up through the snow and felt the bottom of the upper bunk. They were lucky and lived.

I disobeyed orders and broke into the infirmary later that night. There they were—cold, pale corpses, some with eyes still open, five of them at least.

We were ordered to evacuate Portillo, as there was no more food and the railroad had been cut off by fifteen avalanches. I disobeyed orders again and rushed to the front, ahead of our Austrian Ski School–certified guides, who kept exclaiming, "Wait for us! There might be another avalanche!"

I was to be chaperoned by the Ernst Engel family, which had two attractive daughters who were still minors. We went to La Parva, a ski area near Santiago, where I was summoned by Mrs. Engel to play bridge, as they needed a fourth partner.

"What if I want to ski or go climb up the hill?" I asked.

"I'll have you arrested. You're a minor. Do as I say!" was her stern reply. Very Austrian. I was to forget skiing for the entire week, as I had possibly been traumatized.

RIP, Ron Hock from Cornell University. Why has God taken you?

ST. MYNX

MYNX AND I WERE LIVING ABOVE TELLURIDE IN TOMBOY, AN abandoned ghost town, in a dilapidated cabin that we had tried to restore somewhat by peeling the outer wallpaper, whereupon we had discovered the original wallpaper, a golden-colored silk from China. There had probably been a nice teapot and cups from China too, back in the Colorado gold rush of the 1880s.

The Mynx and I had been skiing all summer, from one melting, retreating snowfield to the next, slightly higher. And we had participated in the legendary Lunar Cup, a summer ski race first organized by a madman from Silverton, yours truly.

Telluride had been well represented by its darling, Judy Long DiAngelo, a superb athlete at all sports. The popular Judy was married to the social Jack (J. D.) DiAngelo, who owned property in Placerville, as his well-to-do father, an Albuquerque attorney, loved them both.

At the finish line for the dual slalom, it looked as though Judy DiAngelo would be the winner, as she had led by a wide margin at midway. But at the last minute, the knife-wielding porcupine eater, my girlfriend from Lappland, showed herself to be no slack competitor, as a surge of power put her just an inch ahead, crossing the finish line.

The excited crowd of spectators and fellow ski racers all fell deadly silent. It was as though Hank Aaron, of the Milwaukee Braves, had hit a ninth-inning home run against the New York Yankees, beating them in the World Series in the Bronx in 1956. And yes, I *was* there—as a small child with my great-aunt, who took me to the game when her date stood her up.

The Mynx had just established herself as the most unpopular person in Telluride. I had to intervene before a tar and feathering took place, so we happily left that town to live high up in the cabin in Tomboy. Then, out of nowhere, her concerned parents arrived, wondering just what in the hell we were up to and why their daughter had chosen to follow a madman.

"I am not mad," I said, defending myself—justifiably, as I had won the men's division of the Lunar Cup.

The sliver of a moon and a star rose over the far ridge. Her parents announced that they were driving back down to Telluride, four thousand feet below, and that we should think about just what in blazes we were doing there, living in some kind of a 1860s time warp when miners ate steak.

CONDOR

My flower waits for me
In Bogota
In a stand of carnations
In a single rose
I will place in her hair.
Her love is like
The gentle mountain breezes from Montserrat
A chapel in the Andes.
Her ancestors rode horses over high Andes passes
To Cajamarca, headwaters of the Amazon,
Sailed ships to Cartagena on the Pacific.
She is like the
Shining snows of Huascaran and Huandol
And I am like
A lone condor
Searching for my mate.

HOMELESSNESS AND THE GREAT PAPER EMPIRE

WHEN I GRADUATED FROM HIGH SCHOOL IN **1966,** MY ELDERLY landlady, Goldie Chase, gave me three pairs of underwear for a graduation present. In Hollywood, California, some children received sports cars, but most North American children were lucky to get lunch and dinner. Food consumed more than 20 percent of the family budget even back then. I got a job with Ford Hubbard building clay tennis courts, which paid me two dollars per hour, which was actually more than I was worth. Hubbard went out of business four years later, much to the pleasure of his competitor, Tamarack Tennis Camp, a.k.a. New England Tennis Courts.

I didn't plan on being homeless; I was evicted by Goldie at the insistence of her grandnephew, who also boarded with her and snarled at me whenever she left the living room. I had a sufficient paycheck and a new ten-speed bicycle to get me to the tennis barn every morning at six o'clock. I liked the work, as it would help build my muscles (while slowly destroying my young, strong back) for Alpine skiing, my passion. I had been chosen for summer ski camp with the US Ski Team in Bend, Oregon, on Mount Bachelor, at almost nine thousand feet.

Bob Beattie, the head coach, was a great salesman. "Forward and to the outside," he told us, explaining that he wanted us to ski just like the American silver medalist Winston William "Billy" Kidd.

Billy Kidd told me confidentially, "Don't speak to Kiki Cutter, the cute, friendly fifteen-year-old. Bob has a crush on her." That was funny, but I talked to Kiki because no one else dared to.

At thirty-four, Bob was still a handsome young man with his blond hair cut short like a marine. I don't think he served, though his every ancestor back to the Revolutionary War did.

Bob stood up in front of the lecture hall and demanded of us, "There's no reason why our young American men and women cannot compete equally with our European rivals, the Austrians, French, Norwegian, Swiss, or Germans. We have the talent, and our God-loving country has financial resources sufficient for us to compete in Alpine skiing globally ..." On and on he went. It was spellbinding. We were like Christian soldiers marching into a Crusade, though Bob was no Charlemagne.

So I would continue my passion for my chosen lifestyle, skiing, at the bequest of a great man, Bob Beattie, who would find the necessary corporate tax write-offs to sustain us in battle atop the world's mighty mountains. I probably would have been better off following the Jehovah's Witnesses ...

So I raked uneven clay surfaces to lower the crowns and fill the low spots, while Ford Hubbard, cigar in mouth, drove the tiny tractor with its tiny blade, in ninety-degree heat under the blazing spring and early summer sunshine. Did I really have a choice? When you're young and need money to eat, you must work. This is a worldwide phenomenon.

Then every evening, I rode my bicycle to some secluded spot to pitch my tent, eat my food, sleep, and leave. But bears ate my food and ripped up my tent, so I was looking for a solution, as I still did not have rent money. I had plans to fly all over the world at the request of Bob Beattie or my own ambition.

I flew to South America and Colorado. Bob flew me to California to race Jean Claude Killy. I fell on the giant slalom racecourse in the rotten unfrozen snow there in Lake Tahoe in unseasonably warm weather.

I returned to Franconia, New Hampshire, to rake tennis courts every spring and summer. In late summer and fall, I worked at Sel Hannah's farm and was overpaid again at a dollar and a quarter per hour. However, Sel did not go broke, as wealthy Sugar Hill summer people paid above-market prices to shop locally. Sel wore a big straw hat, carried a pitchfork in his hand, and smiled at them while smoking a corncob pipe. He told his daughter, Joanie, that her great-grandparents were Norwegian. She believed him and won a bronze medal at the World Championships in Chamonix, France, in 1962. Of course, there wasn't a word of truth in that, as Joanie learned later in life when she researched her family tree and found them all to be French Canadian and English Canadian. I wish Sel had lied to me. He wanted me to quit my ski racing foolishness and help him with logging, and I was tempted—until his former employee told me that Sel would never pay anyone to go logging. The only log for sure was the one Sel had for his mistress, Nancy, in the vegetable garden. Sel's wife, Polly, had been paralyzed by polio and was bedridden.

I went out west for twenty years, where I married and had children with my wife, Liv, who was later befriended by a Kiwi, New Zealander, who persuaded her to dump me and find someone rich. Before being served divorce papers, I worked as a roofer for the late Peter Thurston of Telluride, who had moved there from upstate New York to marry and get yelled at a lot. Then I worked at a gas station in Copper Mountain, Colorado, and in a lumber yard with the largest chain saw yet invented in Kremmling.

My mother passed away in Florida. Though she had adopted me, she left me some money, which my wife must have thought I was hiding somewhere, though I hadn't yet received it. I signed lots of documents and amassed a huge paper real estate empire of seventy-one properties, but I owed most all the money at substantial interest. What goes up comes down, and in the divorce it was determined that I actually owned nothing but my pickup and a motorcycle, which my wife drove away.

So it was determined by a judge in Breckenridge, Colorado, that I would be required to pay child support of three hundred dollars per month, and that my meager ski instructor wages minus rent would suffice if I didn't eat at all. Luckily the midmountain restaurant at Gorrono Park in Telluride had free relish, mustard, catsup, and mayonnaise, but

I would have to smuggle saltines from the soup lovers in the lunch line. My daughter Mia, age ten, came to visit on spring break, and when she leaned over on the back of my borrowed motorbike, we hit a parked car. Fortunately no one was hurt, but the damage to the parked vehicle was $1,200. Finally I got fired from the ski school. My own father thought it would be best if I returned to New Hampshire, since Michael Burke, who was bragging about screwing my wife, came to my yard sale in Leadville and bought my remaining tools.

So I returned to Sel Hannah's farm, but Sel had just died. Red was leasing it and buying a lot of Monsanto products to kill the weeds and poison half of Sugar Hill. My pay went up to $1.75 and then $2.50 per hour, and I was being overpaid grossly once again. My mother's money finally arrived, at least in monthly installments, and I was able to rent a few meager places that were small and excessively hot in summer. Of course, I had brought my two dogs, Spikey and Helga, with me from Colorado.

JWK, Bodie Miller's uncle Billy, was having problems with his fiancée, a potter named Barbie Tomson, and he wished I'd help him out by stealing her away. She seemed like good bait—intelligent and well educated at UNH—but she babbled incessantly about her various crushes on a variety of local worthless hippies, all of whom were ten years younger than me. After a few dates at the movies, she decided I was too odorous. (My thyroid failure produced a specific odor.) Then there were bicycle outings where my strange odor was observed once again. I kept striking out until I gave her three years of free ski lessons; apparently I stank less in a cold New England breeze. This might have become a lasting friendship if I hadn't developed that odor, which lasted for approximately twenty years until my condition was properly diagnosed and I was given thyroxine, the tiniest of pills, during my incarceration in the State Nut Ward, having arrived there by ambulance with the sirens blaring.

While asleep in my room at the Eastgate Motel, I had experienced a bad dream in which "they," some kind of boogeymen, were definitely after me. I told my dog, JP, to jump through the window, and then I followed him just as the room blew up behind us. Or so I thought ... and told the police at the Littleton police station, who jumped on me and straitjacketed me so tightly that I thought I was having a heart attack, so they took me to Littleton Hospital and put me under armed guard. When the minister of my church arrived to give me last rites, I told him that I had gone down the tunnel and seen Jesus Christ, Our Lord and Savior, all lit up in a wonderful radiance.

"Oh no, you didn't!" he reprimanded me. He quit the church less than a month later.

I was able to sign myself out of my incarceration, which had been less than rosy although the food was good and there was a television. My roommate had lost his frontal lobe in a boiler room explosion, and every afternoon he read the same blank page from the same blank book. An attractive lady about my age pleaded with me to stay and befriend her; she had been in a head-on car accident and jarred her "noggin." But my bill had already topped $6,500, and I had $20,000 in my bank account that the hospital had not yet discovered.

So Jack Fletcher agreed to rescue me from the "funny farm," and thanks to Jack and his cousin who came along to assist, I became a free bird once again, although I wasn't cured. The truth is that the long misdiagnosis of my condition had allowed me to slip into a macabre world of my own isolation and semi-homelessness over several decades, and returning to normal was going to take more than a few weeks. It actually took me about five years to regain about 90 percent of where I had been at age fourteen, when my hyperthyroidism had led me off on a lifelong adventure in the direction of the absurd.

We've all heard in church that our true home is with the Lord in heaven and that we're just temporary visitors on this earth. So this earthly life is a separation from our home with God, and we're all homeless to some extent. Try to keep your sense of humor after you've been thrown out into the streets. If you have a car, you can park at an all-night McDonald's. Have you ever done this? Most of us have, if we missed curfew as teenagers or something similar. Some people live under bridges, and others live in large cardboard boxes or anything they can find. If you're with a homeless friend, gather some sticks and build a fire in a metal trash can.

Three years after I started working at Cannon Mountain in New Hampshire, my rent was overdue at the Gorham Motel there on the corner. My job paid about $900 per winter, so JP and I headed to my godson's apartment at Morning Star Apartments in Concord—up on the Heights, as they call it there. With a car, I could've more easily driven downtown to the Friendly Kitchen for three free meals daily, where no talking was allowed, because there might be fights between ex-convicts and so forth.

I was still trying to keep my meager job at Cannon Mountain and would drive there at 80 mph in my 1996 Malibu, which was held together with bubble gum.

Miller and I had camped out with his friend Long John in the White Mountain National Forest and everywhere else in the north country. He broke into my neighbor's house on Rabbit Hill, thinking it to be my place, and then—calling it Miller Hotel—rented the rooms to his friends. When the owner showed up, he let them all stay an extra week, to everyone's amazement. What a nice guy! He must have been a parent to some wild teenagers himself.

Miller was a great companion and pet sitter for JP, my wonderful dog, who became quite lame in his later years, from age twelve to fifteen. The two of them and Myra, from Honduras, had innumerable adventures on "the hill" in Manchester, a notorious crime ghetto born out of thin air during the pharmaceutical era.

Miller had another girlfriend named Stacey, whose father, Big Rick, had been in a motorcycle gang—Hell's Angels, no doubt—gone to prison, and been through divorce. Big Rick was living in his car at McDonald's in downtown Manchester, but he had developed prostate cancer.

Like Rob the Hammer, my friend in Kansas, says, "It's not an easy life." If you can go to school, stay there as long as possible. If you can get a job, keep it until you find a better one. We tend to think we will always be able to work, but 30 percent of Americans are disabled one way or another, and that statistic refers only to people of working age who would otherwise be working full-time.

Our president is a crook, but so is everybody else. Trying to make a living in modern America is just as impossible as anywhere else the world, a rat race. Good luck to you, my friend. I hope you're home tonight, not working overtime to pay off your credit card, for half the stuff on the shelves in Walmart is junk.

"YOUNG PRO SKI RACER" HARD FAST LIFE IN THE ROCKIES

I WAS A YOUNG PRO SKI RACER WITH THE INTERNATIONAL SKI RACERS Association when I traveled to Aspen, Colorado, in 1972. I was ranked tenth overall and sixth in slalom with winnings of $6,500, which was more than enough to buy a cheeseburger and beer special at Pinocchio's Restaurant, where the waitresses wore short skirts and low-cut blouses for big tips.

Mine had big ones and a friendly smile, probably from drinking from a flask on the job, but that didn't matter to me. She had auburn-reddish hair and told me that her mother was Swedish from Stockholm—actually more Danish, but that was close enough for me. I was homeless, so going home to her trailer was heaven, and she was the goddess herself, though possibly a drinker, but who was I to complain?

Back then, "young pro ski racer" and "young amateur ski racer" were really titles given to anyone who loved the sport of skiing. There was no freestyle, snowboarding, or super giant slalom—just three Alpine events and three gold medals every four years in the Olympics, which was televised. It was the sport of rich white children who went on family vacations, including Christmas, to snow-covered hills where the children mostly skied and the adults mostly got drunk and told wild stories.

Actually it was 1971, the previous year, when I first met Phyllis Garrett, whose parents had moved from Indiana to Grand Junction, Colorado. My homeless winter wandering separated us seasonally, because I still lived in New Hampshire but wanted to live in the West like my rich friend John Stirling, whose parents had just died and left him four million dollars, including land in Florida, apartments in California, more than a hundred acres on Missouri Heights in Carbondale, Colorado, and a small cabin with no plumbing in Aspen, where the ski industry was thriving and tearing up the old wooden sidewalks of its past mining era and replacing them with concrete, even paving the once-mud streets. That was real western clay mud, at least five pounds stuck under each boot sole.

I managed to tip my waitress a hundred-dollar bill, which is like a few thousand dollars now. She was a saloon gal, and in 1974 we moved together to Telluride, where I finally landed a job as a racing director. She worked as a cocktail waitress at a former brothel at the east end of town, where they gave her free drinks but kept her there till 1:00 a.m. or later. Not terribly happy about that, I disappeared into the Sheraton Hotel for five days with Franny, and then Phyllis was not happy about that maneuver.

Of course, I managed to ski every day at my job, as I was the NASTAR (National Standard Race) Pacesetter. Ski racing was the big show back then, and freestylers were all pot-smoking hippie liberals who ate granola, grew beards, and lived in Volkswagen buses.

Without Phyllis's generous rent support, I soon had nowhere to live, so I brought Chandler home to my comfy metal house, which had no heat. Someone had given me a key to it, as the owner was away. We froze together one long night, with a few in-between not-sweaty flashes.

After I used their chain saw to build a pro jump for my racecourse on the NASTAR race hill, the ski area was fined a thousand dollars by the US Forest Service. So I was not going to be rehired for the following winter, but at least they let me know in April. My pay had been meager indeed, as I was considered a crazy skier fool enough to accept carpenter wages (my words).

I had left home young with no college, but I had managed to gain a berth on the US Ski Team by winning the Junior Nationals GS, though only as runner-up in the downhill. Bob Beattie, the US ski coach, became my parental overseer, a job with which he had been decidedly not thrilled. After interviewing me, he had realized I didn't have any maturity whatsoever, that I was mostly a young hound after naked young ladies, though I did occasionally catch one my own age. This stage lasts only a few years before reality sets in and finances overcome hormones.

Phyllis's mother chain-smoked cigars, pipes, or most anything she could get her hands on, especially after work at her home, where she interviewed me, a ditch digger, and was not terribly impressed.

Phyllis's parents bent over backward to get her a respectable job at the post office, but she still loved alcohol and was late to work more than once. I took her binge drinking with my friends from Silverton, refugees from various parts of the world who had wandered into local bars and learned about a young pro ski racer who lived 12,600 feet above Gladstone and might provide lodging for them. To shorten this story, we loaded Phyllis into my car, from the sidewalk where she passed out cold, and away we drove into the night, back up to 12,600 feet elevation, where it sometimes sleets hail instead of snowing in August.

Phyllis's mother was ballistic, but her father was understanding. Phyllis decided to ditch me one evening for Nick Nohava, an ex-convict, until she found out about him. Then she moved into Silverton proper and took a job with some Navajo whose store sold turquoise.

I was sad to lose Phyllis, but really the bottle was destroying her. She went home to never be forgiven by her smoking mother, while her two sisters, Ingrid and Christine, successfully moved out. Then she went to Alcoholics Anonymous and met some heroin addicts who had gone cold turkey because of the New Life Assembly of God. Jesus proceeded to save them all, while they recruited lost, rich hippie children, defrocking them of their trust funds and family inheritances for good cause, which became an exodus to Texas.

I am no longer a young ski racer. I sold my mining claim in Silverton because of thyroid failure, which was quite possibly triggered by drinking spring water, intended for dishes only, that my fellow mom-comrades brought from the nearby, abandoned lead carbonate mine.

I sent some letters to Texas, after visiting Phyllis once in Paonia with my ski friend Racer Rob Mulrenan, who was impressed with her. Rob called me and said, "Well, doctor, you have good taste. She has les Grand Tetons." We were all becoming middle-aged ski bums, which is not such a glorious profession when the snow melts in May.

I never heard from Phyllis, except that she did "return to sender" a Christmas-in-July parcel that I sent her from Lake City, Colorado. A note was attached, something to the effect of, "I am all done with you!"

Twelve years after Phyllis died, I saw an obituary for us all on ancestry.com: "She was a well respected member of the community and her church in West, Texas. She has gone to the angels now to be one of them."

We are looking forward to hanging stars with Saint Phyllis in heaven. Her God-given gift was animal husbandry, for when she preached the Good News of salvation to farm animals, they immediately fell in love and copulated, creating abundance.

Phyllis fell in love and married a Dutchman with blond hair, who sailed off somewhere. She leaves behind a son, Peter; two sisters; and a dog, three cats, and several thousand farm animals deeply in love.

All you Bedouins out there wandering over the hills (like skiers), looking for your stray animals, come home to your Father (family vacation skiing) and hear the Word of God, that he is good.

For in the beginning there was God ...

ELLIE'S AVAILABILITY
FOR GOD

ELLIE HAS DIED IN FLORIDA.

She served on the town of Franconia's chamber of commerce, at the hospital, and in her restaurant, the Dutch Treat, and she was a board member of just about everything.

The priest asked about her great ability: Was it her accountability or sustainability or credibility? What pleased God most was her availability.

She was always available to serve God.

So a plaque in her honor will be hung on the wall there.

The struggling little town was never a sleepy town in her lifetime. She accomplished a great deal, and everything hummed with the noise of a strong economy. But without God, it would not have been, because the author of it all is … Well, you guessed it. God.

If you will be born again of the Holy Spirit, then everything is possible. For without it, what does it matter? When love fails, there is only despair and destitution.

So, like Ellie, raise yourself up to God to dwell among the angels in the New Jerusalem. A place is prepared there by our Lord, who reciprocates. So, yes, love your God, and you will not be forgotten on earth as well as in heaven.

God rules still. Why would you doubt this and make up your own rules, and then fall into disfavor and infamy? No one is greater than our God. Serve the Lord Almighty, whose government is eternal without end. Peace be with you forever.

Now Hadie, Ellie's cook, has died as well. Peace for her as well in heaven.

ST. CARLA FROM SUGAR HILL

CARLA DEPARTED HER MIDSIZE AMERICAN CAR VIA THE BACK window after it struck a tree at seventy miles per hour—or slightly faster, maybe eighty? Luckily in the car behind her was a medic named Nube (which means "Cloud"), who had been born in Buenos Aires but moved to Boston as a child. Someone phoned 911, an ambulance was summoned, and more medics arrived.

Carla survived, but she had been badly traumatized by her drunk driving episode, which made all the newspapers. Six years later, after completing all the alcohol abuse rehabilitation programs, she got her license back and drove to the Dutch Treat in Franconia, where she met a man whom she thought was Father Time because his beard reached his sandals. Jack took her home to his mother's house on Sugar Hill, explaining that no, he had not just come down off LSD. In fact, he had never stopped taking LSD, plus he had written all of ZZ Top's songs. Carla must have thought him most amusing indeed.

Jack drank a lot of Jack Daniel's whiskey, like his father, who had also consumed a lot of beer and named Jack's brother Sam after Samuel Adams beer—made by their ancestors, no doubt. How original.

Alcoholism seemed rampant in the family, but Sybil, the mother, stayed away from the hard stuff. She preferred wine, wine, and more wine, and then perhaps to dine and with that, please, more wine! Luckily Sybil could cook and had taught Jack to help out, and Carla loved the home-cooked dinners—with wine, of course, because Carla had fallen off the wagon almost immediately. So Carla was there several weeks, and Sybil suggested that Jack and Carla move into the house next door where Jack had lived previously.

Jack had gone skiing every day without Carla, and so when I arrived as a houseguest for an evening meal, I suggested that Jack could teach her how to ski, but he said, "You teach her," looking at me, and that's how Carla became my girlfriend.

So I took Carla across the border into Quebec, because I told her the French made love differently up there, and when we arrived, she could speak fluent French. Boy, was I surprised. *"Merci beaucoup. Je t'aime!"*

I think I lived up to my reputation in Quebec, but upon returning to New Hampshire, I made the mistake of taking her to my newly constructed home, which was sort of like a sugar house without the maple syrup and candy. The walls were large plastic sheets that flapped incessantly in the spring breeze upon the high hilltop. It was a few days before Easter.

Somehow we survived New Hampshire's four-foot blizzard of blizzards. The snow kept falling all night and into the next morning, and the perfect storm—as they are often called—left snow up to my armpits. The governor declared an emergency; all cars were to stay off the road while bulldozers and road graders connected towns as soon as possible.

Carla seemed to enjoy sleeping in. She had a small Pekinese dog, Marguerite, and a cat, Tabby, that made awful messes so she gave it away to some people who had seven already and must have liked that smell.

She found us a bigger and much warmer home, but then she announced that she had a new boyfriend who was closer to her own age and had a dick that stayed harder longer—evidently forty-seven minutes, as she kept time. I usually screwed and fell asleep to avoid Viagra heart attacks.

Finally she discovered that her newfound stud was two-timing her, so she let me move back in the adjoining room as long as I promised not to bother her. Well, women are just better organized than men. My uncle had once told me how women have different priorities and are just plain smarter. Carla announced that we would not be having any more sex. We spent entire evenings mostly playing cards with her dealing, and if I tired of cribbage, then she played solitaire.

That's when I decided to tell her I'd been adopted, and amazingly, so had she. So we decided to buy laptops and hunt down the identities of our biological parents, and their parents, and all their parents. It was endless and a whole lot of paper, you know—notebooks all the way up to the ceiling. One of her ancestors had run away from the burning White House in the War of 1812, while my twenty-seventh grandfather had united Spain, then run out anyone who disagreed with the Catholic church, so all those people had come to the New World, America!

Carla particularly liked playing card games such as gin rummy, and she always beat me, which made her day and explains why our relationship lasted almost two years. Then I suddenly beat her at chess, stood up, laughed, and screamed, "Checkmate!"

That was definitely the beginning of the end, but I had endured so many defeats. She met her fiancé, a younger and faster night ski racer named G. P. Houston, and I was told to move out since he would be moving in. And since all my clothes would fit him, and since she had bought them all, I moved out wearing just my jock strap and a T-shirt.

Jack said his mother wouldn't mind if I moved up there for seven weeks as long as I did the dishes, so I did. I applied for my US passport and boarded a ship for Buenos Aires to see Nube, who had saved Carla many years earlier.

The immigration people in Argentina couldn't spell my name, so they had me pick an Argentine name, something like Spangl Mengele Eichmann. So everywhere I go down there, people throw rocks at me, thinking I'm Adolf Hitler.

"No rocks, please. Just tomatoes," I insist.

Carla, oh Carla, where have you gone? Are you still there in that factory town in New Hampshire? I'm here in Patagonia, where the wind always blows.

Jack's father has died and left them all an inheritance, so he'll be coming here to visit Butch Cassidy's outlaw home, here in Chubut Province, and Sam will be bringing all his dogs in crates to hunt ducks in Cordoba.

I miss you, Carla. Where did the years go?

ST. ANDREA

ANDREA WAS SEVENTEEN WHEN I FIRST FEASTED MY EYES UPON her tiny morsel of a student's body. She had fallen for a friend of mine named Jack Black, who lived on top of Sugar Hill with his mother, Sybil. The petite Andrea had dazzling, sharp-tongued intelligence and wit, perhaps necessary for survival for every runt of a litter. Born small with less physical defense capability, she made up for it—and then some—in other ways. Andrea was an excellent conversationalist, as was Cindy, whom I shall mention in a later chapter. These smart girls were obviously trained well at home by smart mothers.

Andrea had been adopted by some close neighbors down the street from me—actually in Greenwich, Connecticut, the next town over. Fortunately her adoptive parents had money and thus could send her to a nice private school for the rich, where her brother knew Martha Moxley, who would be bludgeoned to death with a golf club the day before Halloween. Even worse, the murder remained unsolved; the older brother, Thomas, who was originally a suspect, was cleared by a lie detector (polygraph) test, but the younger brother, Michael, who had probably committed this gross atrocity, went unnoticed and then scot-free.

Andrea was deeply upset by all this as a child, the golf club having actually impaled Martha Moxley's head. It was indeed ghastly and horrific and no one felt safe with a murderer at large. So Andrea's mother made a plan to send her to White Mountain School, formerly called St. Mary's when my girlfriend Penelope had attended the school there on Turtle Ridge, in Sugar Hill, New Hampshire, years earlier.

There in the White Mountains of New Hampshire, Andrea somehow met Jack Black. With a beard all the way to his toes, he looked like Father Time, except that back then, young Jack was more redheaded than gray.

Jack had more experience—much like Jimi Hendrix—with drugs, mushrooms, and LSD than the petite Andrea, who was now to be introduced to her new lifestyle. Within a year they were married, as she was legal at eighteen, going on nineteen. She joined Jack the Black Pirate on his—now *their*—fishing adventure around the Hawaiian Islands, where the expected child was born but died a crib death at sea. The awful and terribly untrue rumor that spread around Franconia and Sugar Hill was that Jack had taken too much LSD and passed out on top of the child.

The mother, Andrea, was heartbroken and traumatized, but Jack persuaded her to help him pick some mushrooms on Mauna Loa. They added some peyote buttons, and after ten hits of LSD—*hoolaulea!*—a second child was born weighing ten pounds five ounces. They named her Erin, and she was larger than a football and much tougher. With red hair like Jack's, she resembled a Norse goddess engraved on a Viking ship about to plunder Rastafarian Jamaica.

I had the pleasure of taking Erin, between my knees, on her first ski lift ride. Andrea hadn't quite fathomed how to do it, but she caught on immediately, and I never rode up the lift with Erin again. Mother knows best!

Sybil bought them a house next to hers, but deeper into the mysterious woods. Being hippies, they wanted to be far away from everything, there in Jack's Garden of Eden where he grew a lot of beans on his beanstalk. Andrea was deeply in deep love.

But Jack kept shutting off the electricity, and they would argue and fight incessantly, usually over money, as the woman wants it all. All of it! Well, I suppose their fighting was kind of a Viking thing: fighting for the sake of fighting, just so they could kiss and make up until well after midnight and then have sex until dawn.

At one of those all-out atmospheric disturbances, I was hiding in the basement under a pile of wood when I suddenly found Andrea hiding a few feet away. She whispered, "He doesn't know where I am—or where you are, for that matter."

Then I heard the basement door open at the top of the stairs, and Jack, stark naked except for his beard to his toes, yelled, "I know you're both down there. I've searched the house and woods for two miles with no sign of either of you, so you must be there!"

"Why don't you get a divorce?" I asked the fair, petite Andrea.

"We're not even married," she replied.

The lights came back on eventually, and dinner was served. Hippy dinner, of course: black peas, lentils, buckwheat, long brown rice, dandelion greens salad with vinegar dressing, wine made from dandelion greens, plus more LSD! Several days went by before I realized that it was the sun shining through cracks in the organic wall somewhere in the attic.

It was time to go down the hill to see all our friends at Franconia College, where we had signed up to take classes while waiting for scholarships to materialize out of thin air. So we acted just like all those other student bodies floating around. There were quite a few older hippies, who might have been beatniks back in the 1950s heroin outbreak. We realized, of course, that they might indeed be the Hinduism, yoga, and free dance teachers. Group therapy was even a class, though by a different name. Most students were in greater need of a psychiatrist than a teacher, but teachers were a good start and better than most shrinks anyway.

It wasn't too long before Andrea began wandering around, being into all that peace and free love, and she found someone closer to her own age and with a few mushrooms and some LSD. Page was born— another child with amazingly red hair. She, too, looked like a Viking from Iceland or somewhere, and she skied away with Erin. They were off to the Olympics to participate in some way, according to Sybil, who suspected they were following Bode and Ronnie on the World Cup.

Sybil is still mad at Andrea for dumping Jack, her beanstalk son. So Jack moved back into Sybil's house to take care of her and her new husband, Bob, who's some kind of financial genius from New York City and says that Sybil's sons—Jack and the other one, Sam—are both idiots.

"But they're carpenters," I said.

"Same thing as idiots," said financial adviser Bob, the stepfather.

Meanwhile it was rumored that Andrea was looking for yet another catch of the day, as she had gone off with Lobster Bob in his fishing boat down in Massachusetts. Doing ancestry.com, I discovered that Andrea is indeed the descendant of a Scottish pirate named Armstrong who sailed to and claimed the British Virgin Island for the United Kingdom around 1720. And Jack and Sam's ancestor was indeed Samuel Adams, who founded a beer company in Boston that kept all the British drunk during their occupation of Boston during the first year of the Revolutionary War.

The fact that Sybil insists her grandchildren were in the Olympics proves my theory that the grandchildren must have spiked the punch one Halloween. And the fact that hippie parents have created America's most elite, successful ski racers proves that LSD is an antidote to fear. It's also quite helpful for people suffering from chronic depression and/ or trauma, as well as people with illnesses caused by painful memories.

So here we have the proof of the pudding, live from Sugar Hill, New Hampshire, home of Franconia College, where the best thing you can do is forget everything and maybe start your life over by dropping a hit of acid—or nowadays it's more likely ecstasy or another similar drug. Just enjoy life like a hippie, and your children will be much happier for it! Your parents will be thrilled, and we'll all be happy millionaires ... at least in our imaginations.

Andrea was seventeen when I first feasted my eyes upon her tiny morsel of a student's body. She had fallen for a friend of mine named Jack Black who lived on top of Sugar hill with his mother Sybil. The petite Andrea had dazzling sharp tongued intelligence and wit perhaps necessary for survival for every runt of a litter. Born small with less capabilities for defense physically she made up all the difference and then some and was an excellent conversationalist as was likewise Cindy who I shall mention in a later chapter. These smart girls were obviously trained well at home by very smart mothers.

Andrea though had been adopted by some very close neighbors down the street from me actually the next town over Greenwich, Connecticut. Fortunately her new parents had money and could send her to a very nice private school for the rich where her brother knew Martha Moxley who would be bludgeoned to death by a golf club the day before Halloween and what was worse the murder was unsolved as the older brother Thomas who was originally a suspect was cleared by a lie Detector Polygraph test but the younger brother Michael who had probably done this gross atrocity went unnoticed and then scot free.

Andrea was deeply upset by all this as a child, the golf club having been impaled in Martha Moxley's head itself. It was indeed ghastly and horrific and no one felt safe with a murderer at large.

So Andrea's mother made a plan to send her to White Mountain school formerly called St Mary's when my girlfriend Penelope had attended it there on turtle Ridge, Sugar Hill years beforehand.

There in the White Mountains of New Hampshire she somehow met Jack Black with a beard all the way to his toes he looked like Father Time but was not grey back then more red haired and young.

Jack had been more experienced like jimmy Hendrix in the world of drugs, mushrooms and LSD than the petite little Andrea who was now to be introduced to her new lifestyle. Within a year they were married as she was indeed legal at eighteen going on nineteen she joined Jack the Black Pirate on his now their fishing adventure together around the Hawaiian islands where the expected child was born but died a crib death at sea.

The awful and terribly untrue rumor that had spread around Franconia and Sugar Hill was that Jack had taken too much LSD and passed out on top of the child.

Regardless the mother Andrea was heartbroken and traumatized but Jack persuaded her to help him pick some mushrooms on Mauna Loa and they added some peyote buttons and after ten hits of LSD, huala oula a second child was born weighing ten pounds five ounces they named her Erin and she was larger than a football and much tougher as she had red hair like Jack and resembled a Norse Goddess engraved on a Viking ship about to plunder Rastafarian Jamaica.

I had the pleasure to take her up her first ski lift ride between my knees as Andrea didn't quite fathom how to do it but caught on instantly as I never rode up the lift with Erin again as mother knows best!

Fortunately Sybil bought them a house next to hers but deeper into the mysterious woods as they being hippies wanted to be far away from everything in Jack's garden of Eden where he grew a lot of beans on his beanstalk. Andrea was in deep love.

But jack kept shutting off the power, the electricity as they would argue fight incessantly usually over money as the woman wants it all, all of it! Well maybe their fighting was kind of a Viking thing I suppose: fighting for the sake of fighting to kiss and make up well after midnight then sex til the dawn.

At one of these all out atmospheric disturbances I was hiding in the basement under a pile of wood whereupon I suddenly found Andrea hiding a few feet away and she whispered, "He doesn't know where I am, or where you are, for that matter."

Thereupon I heard the basement door open at the top of the stairs, where Jack, stark naked except for his beard to his toes, began yelling, "I know you're both down there. I've searched the house and woods for two miles and no sign of either of you, so you must be there!"

"Why don't you get a divorce?" I asked the fair, petite Andrea.

"We're not even married," was her reply. The lights came back on eventually and dinner was served, of course hippy dinner: black peas, lentils, buckwheat, long brown rice and wine made from dandelion greens, and more dandelion greens in the salad with a vinegar for dressing plus more LSD! Several days went by before I realized it was the sun shining through cracks in the very organic wall somewhere in the attic.

It was time to go down the hill to see all our friends in Franconia college where we had signed up to take some classes while waiting for scholarships out of thin air. So we acted like all those other student bodies floating around! There were quite a few older hippies there that might have been beatniks back in the 1950s heroin outbreak. We realized of course these might indeed be the teachers of Hinduism, yoga, free dance and group therapy was even a class by a different name: most of the students were in need more of psychiatrists than teachers but teachers are a good start and better than most shrinks anyway!

It wasn't too long before Andrea began wandering around being into all that Peace and free Love and she found someone more her own age and with a few mushrooms and LSD Page was born another child with amazingly red hair also she looked like another Viking from Iceland or somewhere and she skied away with Erin they were off to the Olympics to participate in some way according to Sybil who suspected they were following Bode and Ronnie on the world cup!

Sybil is still mad at Andrea for dumping her beanstalk son Jack. So jack moved back into Sybil's house to take care of her and her new husband Bobho is some kind of financial genius from New York City who says Sybil's sons Jack and the other one Sam are both idiots,

"But they're carpenters," I added.

"Same thing as idiots," said financial advisor Bob.

Meanwhile it had been rumored Andrea had gone for yet a new catch of the day as she had gone off with Lobster Bob in his fishing boat down in Massachusetts somewhere. doing ancestry.com I discovered Andrea is indeed the descendent of a pirate from Scotland named Armstrong who sailed to and claimed the British Virgin Island for the UK in around 1720.

Jack and Sam's ancestor was indeed Samuel Adams who founded a beer company in Boston that kept all the British drunk there during there occupation of Boston first year of the Revolutionary War.

The fact that Sybil insists her grandchildren were in the Olympics proves my theory that the grandchildren must have spiked the punch one Halloween. And the fact that hippy parents have created Americas most elite successful ski racers proves that LSD is an antidote to fear and besides it treats very well those people with chronic depression and those stymied by trauma as well as many with illnesses caused by painful memories. So here we have the proof of the pudding live from Sugar Hill, NH, home of Franconia College: where the best thing you can do is forget everything and maybe start your life over by dropping a hit of acid or nowadays it's more likely ecstasy another similar drug. So just enjoy life like a hippy as your children will be much happier for it! Your parents will be thrilled and we will all be happy millionaires at least in our imaginations.

MARTA'S HOUSE

AT MARTA'S HOUSE, SHE WAS BECOMING UPSET ABOUT THE EVENTS to come, while I, never having experienced volcanic eruption firsthand ... Well, I was no consolation and had no useful experience. She was battening down the hatches, blocking out all sunshine by covering the windows with shutters, and our entire rekindled relationship went into the darkness too. We were forbidden by radio and television from venturing outdoors. Eventually we lost electricity, as the metal roof was being pelted by sand, which sounded like rain.

Forty hours later we ventured outdoors to the beach—at least it looked like a white sand beach, but a gooey substance covered everything. The news on the battery-run radio said, *"Bariloche es aislada"* (Bariloche is isolated). The national guard would be called out, and owners of four-wheel-drive vehicles would be asked to truck hay to the starving animals whose grasslands had been covered. Ash even made it to the Buenos Aires airports, closing them down nine hundred miles away.

Wearing a mask, I began the filthy job of cleaning Marta's roofs. I was a roofer and had done other filthy jobs, but I was tracking sand into the house. After eight days of this, Marta had had enough. Obviously, she said, I was not a good person in an emergency, and so I had to leave the next day. I explained that I had only twenty dollars, to which she replied that maybe I could get some money wired—but still I had to leave, so I left. I hooked my luggage and ski bag together and dragged it down the volcanic-sand-covered street to the bus stop, where I met my good friend the restaurant puppy, who had shared my fortune, my meal, and now shared my misfortune as well, with the volcanic ash-sand covering everything, including my luggage.

I bid farewell to him and boarded the bus for the downtown Bariloche bus station, where I took a bus for Esquel, two towns to the south, where the volcanic dust had not yet reached. Esquel was not an overly friendly town, though the hostel was clean, friendly, and relatively unoccupied. So I took many bus rides to the neighboring town of Trevelin, but that wasn't adventurous enough, so in my search for skiable snow, I boarded the bus for Corcovado and Carrenleufu.

KILLINGTON WORLD CUP SANDWICHES

M Y NURSE DIDN'T UNDERSTAND WHY I WANTED TO RUN ONE hundred times around the small, enclosed outdoor space afforded to a few privileged inmates of the sanatorium known as McLane's in Belmont, Massachusetts. I wanted to win the Junior National Ski Championships, and soon did.

"I am a skier, and I will ski again soon. I will not be in this place forever!"

After two months of captivity, they let me out on Thanksgiving of 1964. No turkey for me though. I found a small white boarding house in Rutland, Vermont, that looked more like somebody's home. I ate the welcome apples, as I was now out of money, slept snuggly, and hitchhiked to Killington the next morning, almost two months after my seventeenth birthday. There was one lift open to the top of Ramshead, which was open with a seven-inch base composed mostly of gravel and grass. No snowmaking back then, and no World Cup of skiing.

I was quite hungry after skiing two days, so I told the cashier, who told the dishwasher, who had her sell me a hot-dog roll for seven cents. He said, "Kid, just load up that roll with relish, mustard, and ketchup, and chow down!"

I did, and my knotted-up stomach suddenly felt warm, and blood rushed to my shivering feet and hands. Ever since then, I've called anything like a cracker with mustard, ketchup, and relish a "World Cup sandwich," because some of us who finally raced in the World Cup of skiing had to eat those meager morsels.

I remember that now, fifty-five years later, as I watch Mikaela Shiffrin of the US Ski Team racing down Superstar Ski Trail into the winner's circle, with television and movie cameras catching every second and every smile. Many a child, in Vermont and elsewhere, wished they could grow up to be her. She's lucky, and God must be well pleased with her to have put her in the national and international limelight. The United States has never had such a talented skier, although several came close. Although ski racing is not quite the sport it used to be, times have changed for the better for many skiers.

GELANDESPRUNG

WHILE STILL IN HOLDERNESS, I WAS BEGINNING TO HAVE problems with authority. I had overeaten the spaghetti lunch with a large second helping. Then came the after-lunch announcement: because of high winds, the ski team would be practicing cross-country skiing that afternoon.

It wasn't that I didn't enjoy cross-country skiing. But I had a sensitive, nervous tummy that tended not to hold down large lunches after a three-mile run followed by a long, sweaty hill and straight into a bone-chilling headwind at the finish line. In fact, I had blown lunch two weeks in a row, so I decided to skip practice. Maybe I felt the flu coming on—I wasn't sure.

My absence was recorded and, in good disciplinary fashion, I was suspended from the ski team for the week and made to sit out practice in the study hall. I promptly announced to my fellow students that I intended to quit the team, which I did.

The headmaster applauded my decision and confided to me in his office, "Well, son, there's much more to life than skiing. It's a big world out there with a lot of opportunity—especially for people who aren't skiers," he added with a chuckle.

Although I didn't tell the headmaster, I intended to continue competing independently. I still went to the school's rope tow, deep in the woods behind the school, to free ski. The ski jump wasn't being used, so with my friends Bro Adams and Eddie last-name-forgotten, I set a slalom course on the outrun. When we were informed that our slalom wouldn't be permitted, we got permission to build a kicker on the lip and jump with our Alpine skis in what is called *Gelandesprung.* It was a blast. We were all fifteen years old that year.

The ski coach, Bill Clough, told me that if I would return to the team, he would have me jump, slalom, and giant slalom, and he wouldn't require me to do cross-country skiing. I replied, "I'll have to think about it." I was glad the other coach, Donald Henderson, had taken a sabbatical that year to coach in Sweden. In October of the previous year, he had told me that I acted more like a girl than a boy, and I had replied that his teats were much bigger than mine. He had removed his shirt, as we were digging out ski hill rocks on a work crew for which I had volunteered, instead of playing football, to get brownie points. The hell with him, I had thought, and played football my remaining years there, which I loved more.

I wanted to race the Baxter Cup state qualifier for the Junior Eastern Championships, and I waited by the school van at 6:00 a.m. but then was informed that all the seats were taken by ski team members so I wouldn't be going. Then two kids didn't show up, so the coach reluctantly agreed to let me go to that race in North Conway. I had to beat my teammate Ned Gillete to win that race, as well as Dennis Ostermaier, whose parents managed the Mount Ossipee Skiway in Ossipee, New Hampshire.

So I qualified to race in the Junior Eastern Championships at Jay Peak, Vermont, on Presidents' Day weekend, which was a school holiday. Fortunately my father drove his Italian sports car to the school to pick me up. He was wearing a big fur coat and drinking brandy from a flask, and off we went to Jay Peak, the stateside, which had two long T-bars back then.

It was twenty-six below zero, but it had warmed up from thirty-five below. We had metal skis and leather boots back then, which became more and more wet all day long, until finally your toes could take no more—which luckily happened about the same time the lifts shut down and the sun set, around four in the afternoon, maybe five by February. My own father said he had never been so cold in all his life, that he could remember, as he volunteered to be a gatekeeper to get a free ski ticket and watch the race.

My teammate Terry Morse, who was a year older and from Aspen,

Colorado—I didn't know him well, because he was buddies with Bill McCollom, another older teammate—got going so fast on the upper section, with his Sohler Blue Bird downhill skis, handmade in Germany, that he veered off the course, catching an edge and flying straight into a birch tree, a branch of which was sticking through his broken jaw when they found him. They had to cut the branch from the tree and carry it along with Terry to the hospital, but first load him into a toboggan and keep him alive. There was a lot of blood.

Of course, this delayed the ski race until almost sunset. Meanwhile the wind blew at fifty miles an hour, and my father stood there motionless on the side of that mountain in his fur coat, emptying his flask and leaking profanities: "Damn cold, damn cold, damn cold," plus a few other choice words that I wish not to repeat. Waiting higher up the mountain in even more wind, I probably was wearing two sweaters that day, but ski clothes were not as warm in that ancient era as they are now, which was the reason for my father's fur coat, the other reason being that the damn heater in the sports car didn't work well. But it really was a fun summer car, my father would interject as he yelled at the heater to work, followed by another nip from the flask. People generally drank and drove back in those days, unlike nowadays, when it means prison for anyone caught. Back then it was a matter of the judge's discretion, meaning that for a few hundred dollars—two or three weeks of pay—one could get the charges reduced.

At any rate, I was so cold by the time I stepped into the starting gate that I didn't do well at all, finishing in thirty-fifth place, at the bottom of the pack. Luckily my feet didn't freeze off, but I had to soak them in cold water for forty-five minutes, which made me shiver without end until I crawled under huge blankets at the motel, which furnished extra electric heaters for every room. I had never slept so well.

Back at Holderness Prep School, which most of my former classmates referred to as a prison at our thirtieth reunion, I was no hero for my mediocre performance. I went to the ski hill and found that our Gelandesprung lip had been destroyed by the ski jumpers, who had begun practicing anew. Warmer weather ensued in March, and by April all the snow had melted in a violent rainstorm called mud season in the sticks. (Trees without leaves were referred to as sticks, lol.)

The next year I was back there in Holderness, that prison for the children of wealthy parents who had better things to do than raise them. I flunked English by not writing a term paper that my roommate had even volunteered to dictate to me so that I wouldn't fail the subject. Then it was decreed by that same awful Headmaster Hagerman that I would not be allowed to compete in the Junior Eastern Championships because I had flunked English.

I went into a slight rage and threw my chair through the window of our room, in which the temperature quickly dropped to match the outdoors temperature of ten degrees. My roommate, Robert Childs, moved to another, warmer room.

Technically I was expelled from the school, and a letter was sent to my father's office informing him to come pick up his unruly child in the freezing room, where I was told I would have to pay the carpenter's bill of $239, which would take me all summer.

My father was driving around in his fur coat somewhere, maybe Long Island, which had the Sound to protect it somewhat from New England cold fronts. Nevertheless he took his flask with him in the inside pocket, as was fashionable in those days.

I began reading *Anna Karenina*, Ibsen, Camus, Voltaire, and Dostoevsky at my stepmother's suggestion to do something with myself until my father arrived to retract me. He wasn't happy to have spent so much money on my failed education, as he informed me, scolding me to tears on the long drive back to Connecticut. But finally he asked if I had learned anything at all from the entire awful experience, and I confessed, "Gelandesprung!"

"What exactly is that, a foreign dish?" he inquired.

Within two years I had an opportunity to fly again to Portillo, Chile, for a competition that they were rigging to be won by Othmar Schneider, the ski school director and Olympic slalom gold medal winner.

"Let Othmar win this event," the ski school instructors told me. "He'll be awfully mad if he doesn't win."

Of course I won, outjumping the hill but not falling despite a hard landing on the flat.

Then in 1977 my good buddy Ned Mulford, who owned Paragon

Sports in Telluride, informed me that he was going to participate in a Gelandesprung contest in Crested Butte. Was I interested in competing for money? We'd be jumping over a road with vehicles so as not to slow down on the in run and collide with a bus, and so on.

Ron Barr, son of an Aspen grocer and former University of Denver and US Ski Team member, was winning most of those events largely on style points awarded by judges onto total distance of each skier's jump. It was a blast, with screaming spectators and a great format. The lead skier in the first jump jumped last in the final jump and usually won the contest, with the eyes of every spectator upon him. Twenty years later this same format was adopted by F.I.S. World Cup Skiing, who reversed the finish of each first run's top thirty-two racers to have the champion of the first run coming down the hill last, with all the spectators cheering like at today's Killington World Cup.

I never managed to win another Gelunde, as we began calling them. I was third at Aspen behind speed skier Tommy Simmons and Ron Barr again, and fourth at Durango, where Billy Kenney (Bode Miller's uncle) went upside down, going out of our sight from the top. He landed so hard that he shit his britches, which had to be peeled and cut off him with scissors the next morning at the Telluride home of Becky Bonnet and Maty Kay Waugh, where we had taken him, as there was still some sign of life. The next year at Purgatory, near Durango, another Gelande contestant did that same jump and slid out on the outrun, but he was found dead with a broken neck. That was the end of that three-year professional Gelundesprung Pro Tour, as there was a huge lawsuit of one million dollars.

I had gone to Jackson Hole for that Gelandesprung earlier that year. I had the phone number of a French blond named Sandy Seusse, who had really thick glasses. She escaped her mechanic boyfriend to meet me just past midnight for what turned out to be an all-night sex orgy. Having rarely seen women during my three long, depraved years at that Holderness prison, I wanted desperately to make up for lost time, so we repeated three times our interlocked union—or was it five times? Suddenly there was daylight, and I had to get to the jumping hill for the pro event. I launched on my second jump, although a bit nervously, as I had almost fallen on my first jump. Then, without warning, I did the Billy Kenney—went over backward midair and landed with a great crash, upside down and headfirst into the transition, sliding almost lifelessly onto the outrun.

I remember Sandy, the young lady, screaming from the sight of so much blood. My eyes rolled back in my head, so I must have looked dead. Then I came to and tried to stand up, but immediately fell over. More screaming. Somebody asked me what year it was, and I said 1962—off by fifteen years. My girlfriend, Cindy Wright, arrived from out of nowhere, but luckily Sandy had gone off to work as a waitress.

"Who are you?" I asked my steady, not recognizing her. She ended up not marrying me, but she found a new boyfriend with millions who had a more stable lifestyle and steady job counting his money, not his gelunde exploits.

The years have flown by, but I still dream that I'm doing that extra jump at the end of the steamboat competition on Howelsen Hill, where I finished fourth. I went back up the hill, climbed into the shrubs and small trees above the start ramp, and came onto the in run already going twenty-five miles an hour. When I hit the lip, I split my tips apart like a modern-day jumper—twenty years before it became the style—and sailed 220 feet, landing in the transition and outjumping the hill with one last exhibition jump. I guess I was a born entertainer. Now I go to karaoke instead, but I'm not very good, maybe fourth or fifth. Every racehorse has his day.

DAWNLEY

I LOADED MY TWENTY-ONE DOGS INTO MY FORD F150 EXTENDED-CAB pickup, where they filled most of the front and back seats. Then me and the Dalmatians drove to Colorado; since their lives and mine too were possibly in danger, it was the right decision for all of us.

I had yet to inform my faraway fiancée that she was indeed a fiancée, so I asked for her hand in marriage as we were driving east from South Fork, Colorado, a town made famous in the Chevy Chase movie *Vacation*, in which the cabin falls down when the door slams and the dead grandma is tied to the roof rack.

And her reply, because she had wanted to marry her last boyfriend but he wouldn't ask, was, "Yes, I want to get married, indeed!" Much better than me. How had I pulled it off? So we drove to Taos, filled out a marriage license, and then went straight to the Santa Fe Marriage Chapel, where Dawnley opted for the shorter civil ceremony—and it was done! She was forty-six years old, still slender and good-looking. I'm not sure how I pulled it off, but maybe it was just good timing.

At the motel later, it was a different story, as she claimed a headache. Then within two days her lesbian bisexual girlfriend showed up with a boyfriend, and we all went motel hopping from Alamosa to Salida to Gunnison.

The Dalmatians had gone deer hunting from my cabin one night; fortunately they could take care of themselves. Then at Thanksgiving, Dawnley's ex-husband, Scott, showed up with her child Tyler, and we enjoyed a great feast in Montrose, where I not-too-candidly announced, "I guess we're one big happy family now."

Scott had quit drinking, but the cure and all its pills were worse than the disease, as his temper kept flaring up at my every suggestion.

"Tyler has a girlfriend, and she's a guitar player and sings," announced Dawnley, having polished off her daily twelve-pack of beer plus a few tiny bottles of whiskey. So we all went to Scott's house, where the girlfriend showed up and sang better than Joan Baez or Carly Simon. Then Dawnley and I left the party, only to hear the next day that Scott had asked Tyler's girlfriend to leave and slammed the door on her guitar-strumming fingers, chopping them off at the ends.

"Bad drugs they've given Scott," I concluded, but that wouldn't grow her fingers back.

"Well, he always had a problem with his temper," added Dawnley.

Seven years later, Scott was schussing down Telluride when he swerved to avoid a child, caught an edge, and collided with a tree. He was pronounced dead on arrival at the medical clinic.

Dawnley wakes up every morning in the Mountain Village employee housing complex, where she lives to this day, and pounds two beers for breakfast. Sometimes she eats, but it's usually at work at the Conoco gas station and delicatessen at the bottom of Lawson Hill. She used to bicycle after work, but she's given that up. Now she walks to the nearby liquor store for a twelve-pack and a pint of more firewater.

Dawnley had been adopted in Saratoga Springs, New York, after her father died while she was young. Then the mother, realizing that Dawnley would inherit money only if she finished college, shipped her off to juvenile prison, where she was soon at the mercy of the lesbian guards, who enjoyed their careers and Dawnley as well.

Her son, who lost his girlfriend, is now homeless in several western states and has never once held a job, even though his father had taught him painting, both house and auto body.

I wanted to file for an annulment on the grounds that in New Mexico, it was illegal for lesbians to marry back then, but I never quite had the heart or enough money for a lawyer.

At the age of nineteen, Dawnley was a passenger in a motorcycle accident that resulted in her having a plate inserted in her skull, which is one of the reasons for her drinking. When she's drunk, her back oozes an oily substance that makes giving her a backrub my fondest high priority, as she indeed has a beautiful white Irish body.

She had been the star shortstop on my first wife's softball team, Baked in Telluride. I had been the manager until the end of the season, when they decided to fire me, whereupon the team broke up into squabbling factions, but those young ladies were among the prettiest in the land. Dawnley hit a walk-off homer in one game and we won, but we were no championship team, just all champions in our own hearts.

Still she is my great champion, because when many others had said, "No, I don't think so," she had said the magic words, "Yes, I want to get married!"

GUERNICA, AN INDICTMENT OF UTOPIA

Perhaps it was a spiritual illness
Called Marxism-Leninism
Whose original proponents were possessed
By some industrial demons?

Born in squalid conditions,
These poor imagined there might be a utopia
In some faraway place called heaven on earth,
Where all men and women would be brothers-sisters
In a workers' paradise with huge smokestacks.

Even so, death is required to gain access there—martyrdom.
One needs to be lined up, shot, and buried in a ditch,
So the many poor and homeless were lined up accordingly,
Perhaps given a last cigarette, but more likely their pockets emptied,
Their last cigarettes stolen from them
By men with machine guns claiming to have been sent by the pope.
Whosoever fears for his life fears all these wretches.
Will there ever be justice for the poor, when pigs will fly?

Who is this who claims the right to kill another?
Is he not a devil himself as well?
The rich men are favored by God; they are His anointed,

Chosen to do God's work, to vanquish the
poor for their uncleanliness,
To punish them for their sins,
To cleanse the earth of their iniquities,

Because they are all thieves who imagine
That what is mine or yours should belong to them instead.
Their fingers are sticky like glue, they are corrupted,
They have fallen into an empty hole of atheism,
So let the devil save them if he shall choose to,
Though the devil saves no one; only Christ will save us.

So abandon those who have lost God's blessing.
Planes are coming to drop napalm on them,
To burn into hell all the disbelievers.
Believe instead that God can save your rotten soul,
Your one God who loves you; return to him.
His arms are ready and waiting to embrace you
When you shall return to your cross, ready for salvation.

There may be no mercy for you here on this earth,
But heaven is willing and patiently awaits
Your return to dwell with angels.
Marx was a devil and Hitler his disciple.

I know you thought you deserved a better life,
A better life than the one you reaped.
What you sowed was madness,
Because your own parents were tempted
To lie to you for your protection.

The truth was hidden from you,
That Jesus loves you, no other.
The only gift from heaven, His Eternal Love,
Is all you need to accept—not Marx,

Not Engels, not Mao and Stalin.
So return to Golgotha, come to the cross
Which is prepared for you also,
That where He is in heaven, you may be also,
To be with Him Who loves us.
We are incapable of love, only greed.

Turn away from greed and selfish desire
To serve Him Who sent you here,
To serve lovingly the One who sent you.
Let His love fill your heart with joy.
Be most compassionate and kind,
So that when you see a beggar, give.

Give all you have to give with joy
When they shall ask you for help.
Then you shall rescue them from despair.
They shall all see we are Christians by our
love, charity, hope, and faith.
We who are the merciful are not haughty.

We do not run around with our noses stuck up.
We condescend and make friends
With those less fortunate, with the poor,
The homeless, the orphans, and the widows.
We shall console them in their sorrows and be godly.

We talk of God with gladness.
He loves us all and can save us
From this pit into which we were born.
We will rise up from the ashes.
We will rise up to see Him.

Though we were dead, we shall
Be resurrected by the thought of Him,

Our God, Who loves us, and so we receive
In order to give freely.
This love of His that came to us, we pass it along

To those less fortunate than us; they fill the streets,
They are window shopping on the sidewalks,
Yet what is displayed in windows cannot save them,
Although chocolate goes a long way
To make us more loving and restore us.

It is our God (God's love) Who bakes the cake,
Who kneads the dough and adds the water of life
That it may rise to feed us these fresh loaves of bread.
It is not a right to be fed; it is a privilege of the deserving of the Lord.
Though they sow their fields, the harvest is not guaranteed.
Be thankful for what you have,
And do not imagine you need your neighbor's wife or car as well.

Be content and not led into temptation.
Do not think what others have belongs to you.
Only God is yours, and you are His.
Seek salvation first, and everything shall be added to you.
We are all monks and nuns, fathers and mothers.
We are the stewards of this creation given to us.

Therefore be responsible.
The heathen are not.

O THE HAPPY PINES

Whenever I shall return to New Hampshire,
There the happy pine trees with arms unfolded,
Outstretched long brazen branches like arms
That reach upward as though to embrace the sun
And heaven itself in some kind of a laughter or great joy,
How they greet me, so many happy pines.
Not that the spruces or firs are any less happy or any less green,
But the deciduous trees in winter have all fallen asleep,
Saving their joy for perhaps May until September.
So more it's these happiest of pines I see in winter months too,
With arms unfurled, grasping at heaven in warm embrace
Even though the sun may have just set or still may rise.
What friends I have whose smiles are like unfurled arms of pines,
Whose laughter inspires even the gods,
Who are perhaps no more than the cherubim and seraphim.
Perhaps their arms are like these pine branches, curled upward,
Unfurled downward from heaven somewhere,
For I have miles to drive before I sleep,
And my companion is so asleep inside my oversize down parka.
Somewhere she has gone near the lake's edge on a July afternoon
Beneath so many tall pines in northern New England perhaps,
Or perhaps she is in Colorado or New Mexico or Arizona?
These pine trees seem to be everywhere that trees exist,
So they must be in heaven, too, with my friends who have passed.
Now the white eerie moon arises to illuminate my cruel world.

Many of my pets have passed likewise and died cruel deaths.

Likewise my time remaining here has grown shorter than I can even imagine,

So I must unfurl my arms and reach upward in warm embrace.

I hope there is a reason for all this love that trees express in gentle breezes.

I hope there is a loving God that made these trees to grow and sing their song.

So I must try to sing and hope like the happy pines,

I must try to embrace just as my own mother held out her arms

To hold me close to her breasts, that I may nurture and thrive

Like O these happy pines ...

QUEEN BARBARA
OF SUGAR HILL

FIRST MET THE LOVELY PRINCESS Barbara WITH HER CONSORT, John William "Billy Goat" Kenney, Bodie's uncle, who said to me, "Here, I'll introduce you to Barbara. She's been far too challenging for me, but perhaps she's your type and you can make some sense outta her. It's been a real struggle for me. She is really different, not your run-of-the-mill girl."

Barbara was twenty-eight years old. She was in her pottery shop, a kiln set up on an earthen floor in a shed next to Mark Rich Timber Frame Construction, where Craig Millar worked in two-blocks-long downtown Franconia. She was kicking away at the potter's wheel, making it spin as she was molding a vase or flowerpot or something. "I've always worked," announced Barbara, "and someday it will pay off, I hope."

"Yes," I reassured her, "I build tennis courts for Mike Kenney."

"So you know Billy Kenney?" she asked. "Do you think he's right for me? His mother thinks I should marry him."

So I proceeded to get myself stirred into her murky coffee cup of a mess with Billy. Their relationship had become a big mess because he said he would wait to marry her until *after* the baby was born, as there was no reason to rush into things.

Peg, Billy's mother, had convinced Barbara that they would make an excellent couple. Barbara had been married once before, to a farmer at the University of New Hampshire in Durham, near the ocean, but things hadn't worked out. Her first husband had beaten her physically, and so she was quite traumatized, but back then I didn't realize what trauma does to the brain, even though I too had been traumatized. Barbara and I had that in common, so we were on a path to becoming good friends, if only I could have confessed to her my inner hurt, my feelings, and so on, but I was a hard shell on the outside—and besides, she wanted to do most of the talking.

It turned out, when I researched her family tree twenty years later on ancestry.com, that Barbara was a ninth cousin and my closest relative by blood in all of Sugar Hill. Not only were we related, but she and I both were related to Ferdinand and Isabella, monarchs of Spain, because their daughter had married the Prince of Wales in the United Kingdom of Great Britain.

Of course, at the early stages of our relationship, I did not know any of this, but I sensed that by some unexpected miracle, we belonged together, even though she seemed quite out of the ordinary. We went to the movies a few times, and she insisted on doing most of the talking. I mostly agreed with her, as she would always be right anyway. It was as if she were from the Masonic Lodge, dressed up in a stately costume of the British royalty, wearing a tiara and holding a sceptre that she would wave to make the world a better place, because now she, Queen Barbara, would be in charge, and the subjects had better kneel and pay homage to her commands.

Oh regal queen, I bow before you, so do knight me.

Unfortunately knighthood was not to be mine, because the queen announced to me, "You smell. Don't you know where the deodorant and cologne are? You need some!" I was just a poor homeless waif, a hippie from the forest with no bathroom but the woods, while she, being a queen, had a substantial inheritance plus help from her father, who owned a gas station. So she bought a run-down, dilapidated building in nearby Bethlehem and turned it into her retail castle: big glass windows well lit all night long featuring oriental rugs, glassware, china, furniture, dolls, postcards, jewelry, pottery, and more. You name it and Barbara, the queen of retail, had it.

She had a sweet and gentle side, like candy apples, that not all men were permitted to see, but she displayed all this sweet charm to children, as they were her special field of interest. She would have loved to adopt them all and bring them into her special kingdom, kind of like Michael Jackson, the singer-dancer. She had been trained as a teacher and received a teaching certificate from the University of New Hampshire, near the ocean.

Stephanie Eaton, the politician, and her brother Gordon (Gordi) Eaton of the US Olympic team were also related to us, though more distantly. They were the only other neighbors who I could decipher on ancestry.com as being also related to that wing of royalty attached to the Spanish monarchs—who, as it turned out, were actually the Bourbons of France. Alfonzo of Spain, Ferdinand's grandfather, perhaps had married a Princess Urraca of Portugal, whose mother was actually the wife of the English monarch.

Barbara definitely had an Olympic body, being a Thompson like the current Olympic female champion. She and I bicycled the loop in Franconia that passes the Horse and Hound and Franconia airport, a grass runway for gliders. Then we skied Wildcat, Bretton Woods, and Cannon Mountain, but my health was failing because of slow thyroid, and this makes the body give off unpleasant odors because it can't eliminate toxins quickly enough, so Barbara dumped me and that was that.

One time we hiked to Bridal Veil Falls, and she stripped and jumped in naked, so I felt an equal impulse, but before I actually splashed into the water, she had jumped out and was drying herself. One time we climbed Mount Lafayette with Denise Whipple, the town cop, Ernie's girlfriend, and when Denise and I reached the summit ten minutes after Barbara, who was an avid hiker, Barbara announced, "Well, we have to go down right now. We can't stay, because I have to open my shop. I have bills to pay, so let's get going." Of course we obeyed. After all, she was the queen. It was so typical of Barbara to be off in a hurry and going somewhere.

Her mother hated me at first sight but just adored my buddy Brian Pendleton, who had read a book on how to talk to women, whose brains are different. Perhaps he was charming out of necessity, as he had squandered his inheritance, a trust fund of a few hundred thousand dollars. He had bought two new cars and rolled them over into the woods, driving under the influence. He did rather enjoy himself—dating several blondes, taking them out for fine dining, but mostly drinking at the Cutter Inn in East Burke. Such was Brian's charm that he would subtly listen for queues for handouts or free meals or stacking firewood, while I'm often much more direct.

Someday forgive me, Barbara, for all my hair has fallen out while yours is now gray. But you are lovely still, like the Princess Urraca that you indeed were when we played tennis so long ago.

DOGSTORY
THIRTY-FIVE

MAYBE WE DOGS ARE NOT QUITE AS STUPID AS MANY IGNORANT people think. We lie around on our doggy beds while Thanksgiving dinner is prepared for the entire family. Then the overstuffed, growing children feed us scraps beneath the table, and we accommodate them by helping to empty their plates so that they won't be reprimanded and miss desserts, pies, and ice cream.

Erika, a special woman living in Twin Mountain, New Hampshire, had come from the bombed-out city of Hamburg, which had been decimated by American Flying Fortresses in retaliation for the London Blitzkrieg ordered by Hitler. She had married a Chinese engineer from Hong Kong after the war, and they had settled miraculously in Boston at first, until their separation and divorce after which she brought her children north. Erika liked picking blueberries and entertained a family of bears who delighted enormously in those same bushes, several hundred yards from her cabin there in Twin Mountain on Route Three.

Erika's children had mostly all grown up when my master, Finneus, became acquainted with her. She saved his uneaten portions of food, which she prepared to feed us as well. Waste not, want not!

We dogs are not so logical as humans; we rely more on instinct and intuition. Sometimes at night stars move about in the heavens, and we notice them much more than most humans do. "Extraterrestrial activity" is the term our master Finneus uses to refer to these nocturnal occurrences.

The various retired and resident police in that little police state of a town felt inspired to terrorize us dogs and my master with frequent visits concerning building codes and dog ordinances. The extra stars in space seemed to be listening to every police dispatch and activity, as though it were all some experiment in a test laboratory.

The blond lady with big tetons next door to us ran a day care for young, expectant, possibly police mothers who were of a separate society apart from the general population. The aliens took notice. We often barked through the woods like a wolf pack, sending shivers up and down expectant spinal columns, if not our own.

The friendly older town sheriff took notice of Erika's long blond hair and naked shoulders, hoping for another piece of her apple pie and coffee while listening to her every grievance.

Erika worked part-time at Lovett's Inn, at the bottom of the hill known as Franconia Notch. Charlie Lovett owned it and assisted his ex-navy cook, Pete Trevino, in preparing dinner for 164 more-than-borderline alcoholics who unanimously agreed that a Bloody Mary was a standard summer health drink because it contained an olive, maybe even a small onion or a carrot on the side and a slice of lemon. Someone had to assist in proper nourishment so that at weekend's farewell, these merry revelers would be physically able to steer their cars homeward through the notch to Boston, New York, or Washington.

Erika was hostess, while her son, Austin, mixed drinks and Finneus delivered them to the dining room. My master had perhaps the best job of his ski bum career there, before his somatosis, referred to as male menopause by most. But we dogs are psychiatrists, among other things, and we know exactly—even better than Captain Kohler, chief New Hampshire state police psychologist, who had my master listed as a pot-smoking, paranoid-schizophrenic hippie, even though his hair was not below his shoulders.

It was very much a secret state within a state, this Twin Mountain, which had a collection of business owners who had moved there from mostly Massachusetts, probably to avoid taxes and possibly to hide out from the known world under the watchful eyes of cameras above every traffic light, and so on.

Probably this was all just a reflection on the national government, which had cameras and eyes all over the world watching everybody and everything. As long as there was dog food, we dogs didn't seem to mind at all, and we felt safe knowing that even Captain Kohler was being monitored from space for his noticeably strange behavior toward everyone, including Finneus.

WHAT PEANUT BUTTER DID TO MY MORTAL HUMAN BODY

66 **P**EANUT BUTTER IS DELICIOUS," SAID MY FATHER.
I was a picky eater as a child, plus we were going to a tropical country where the salads were full of microbes. Thus we bought peanut butter canisters weighing five pounds each.

I was more than four years old when I began eating mostly peanut butter and a predominantly vegetarian diet. I loved olive oil, sunflower oil, and all things from the plant world. My father was a traveling salesman and took me all over the world with him, as my mother had died and a governess would be more expensive in the United States than in third-world countries such as Colombia, where breakfast consisted of every imaginable fruit on our planet.

My father tried to persuade me to eat something other than peanut butter, but since the fish in tropical markets still had their eyes, I felt guilty eating them—or guinea pigs still alive in burlap sacks in Peru. How could anyone eat them, or choose to eat *any* living animal?

I preferred pineapples and decaffeinated coffee with boiled hot milk.

In Paraguay, I drank too much yerba mate before my father realized it was full of caffeine, which made my heart race and his too. We raced around everywhere, even to Tierra del Fuego, the land of penguins. I could not imagine eating penguins, although I was told that Mapuche and Araucanian Indians boiled them in stew.

I preferred my peanut butter, and I grew up on it until my college days at the University of Cameroon, which is in Africa, the land of peanuts and lima beans. I preferred those, too, and anything with large quantities of vegetable oil.

I fell in love with a young woman who preferred eating mostly pork chops, lamb chops, and beef brisket. Our marriage didn't last long, but our children were quite well balanced, consuming everything in sight except the refrigerator itself.

The years flew by and I ate mostly peanut butter still, to the dismay of my now-grown-up children, who thought my continuance of the peanut diet might be altering my body chemistry. Perhaps they were correct, as I was eventually diagnosed with a brain disorder of some indistinguishable type. My psychiatrist gave me a brain scan and told me confidentially, "We don't often see this kind of phenomenon in humans. You are quite peculiar in that your brain waves are more similar to those of plants, specifically evergreen trees and evergreen shrubs. Do you celebrate Christmas at home the entire year?"

"I'm no Santa Claus!" I protested, feeling quite insulted by all of this. "But I do take long walks in the forest behind my house. There are many pine trees and spruces, balsam fir and a few cedar trees and shrubs. It is very damp and beautiful; and yes, I do consider the trees to be my friends. I even speak to them, but they do not reply in human words. I'm no schizophrenic hearing voices, if that's what you mean to imply. The trees have their own language, which is more like ESP or telepathy. They feel love for each other and even for me, but they do not love any lumberjack out there to murder them or their cousin trees."

I soon gave up on that psychiatrist and took even longer walks in my forest, to the further dismay of my close friends and associates—except for one good fellow, a biologist, but he died shortly thereafter.

Palm trees and deciduous trees never were close to me, and I'm not sure why. I do eat peanuts still on all my daily and increasingly nocturnal adventures. I walk barefoot nowadays as well, not certain exactly when this began, but I'm enjoying feeling my toes sink deeper and deeper into the wet topsoil.

I think I shall never return to the human rat race and its preoccupation with destroying our planet via industrialization. I am most comfortable here in my forest, among trees who have proven to be my best and most long-lasting friends on this earth—especially the evergreens, but now increasingly every tree and bush and plant.

I wiggle my toes deeply into the earth, but now they will not move. They just stretch deeper and deeper, so I raise my arms higher and higher, up into the stars, moon, and sun …

A LOGGER'S REMORSE

Menorah-shaped bushy treetops of
These lovely pines in their silent constant prayer,
How could anyone of right mind
Cut down a living tree?
Far worse than kidnapping or blasphemy
Is the logger's quota in board feet,
And the mill itself with jagged saw teeth is a hungry devil possessed.
Because these pines and firs stand like sentinels,
Guardians of our mother, this planet Earth,
Waving their long arms at us with every passing breeze.
So my entire young manhood was wasted clutching a chain saw,
As though I were achieving some great purpose
More than sheer obsessive destruction of the Earth itself.
This giant chain saw in hand, I, the mighty tyrant,
Whose marriage was soon doomed by God Himself intervening.
And now the birches themselves sprouting buds …
It is mid spring, and these woodlands
All shout with joy and benediction and praise.

DEAR DAD

to Louis

Dear Dad, a.k.a. Father,
I realize we have never understood each other perfectly
Because I am an arrogant, insolent, disobedient, rebellious child, and
Sometimes I even imagine you were one also
in your own day in your own way.
Since I am created in your own image, please do inform me,
Just exactly where did I go wrong?
I do remember cutting down the apple tree for
firewood and burning it in the fireplace
Because I was cold, and yes, I made an apple pie and ate that too.
Was it the apples themselves, or was it unkosher to eat the fruit too?
I should have planted them all, that they might become an orchard?
So you banished me from the family farm
on Cider Hill deservedly. Hmm ...
Well, I began to dream and pray that you might remember me,
Remember that you took me on weekend ski
adventures on sought-out peaks!
Your holy mountain, I suppose, was
whichever one had the most snow
And biggest cloud with constant snow
flurries, but then it would rain also
So that some weekends we would stay home and save money

To not see all those other holy people high
up there on that sacred hill.
Now, because I long for those days to return,
I am called a weatherman like you.
I try to predict where the snow will fall and where
all those followers of skiing will appear.
Some of them had their own mountains somewhere
else and were not part of our congregation.
Therefore I conclude that they were of some different persuasion,
Yet we were true and loyal followers of the
snow, which fell like holy manna.
Remember too that we tried to eat it with maple
syrup during that ski race at Stowe.
Now I write to you and beseech your forgiveness, as you
are older than me with one foot already in heaven.
Dear Dad in heaven, perhaps in your dreams
you are already there somewhere.
I am sure it's a better place than the Mississippi River,
although they are trying to clean it up, an impossible task.
That is why we prefer mountains, etc., because
sewage runs off with gravity somewhere.
I would rather not concentrate on that, but instead
upon what is more holy and higher up.
You, Father, administered and managed my
childhood to make it a heavenly experience
So that when I finally leave home, I might be
able to manage my own household.
My Father in heaven, hallowed be thy name.
Thy kingdom come. Thy will be done.
To save it from destruction and decay, debauchery and filth.
With that in mind, I think of you in fond remembrance
Of the fine cutlery at home, the Dutch plates
and saucers, cups and glasses.
Yet those material things are nothing
compared to your spiritual oversight.
My father in heaven! Hallowed be thy name, thy kingdom
come and thy will be done on earth as well.

FREEBOX TOO

Then I went to the freebox (time number 934)
With some old clothes to discard.
Used often, now I no longer need them, but fold them
Out of respect, for they served me well and might yet serve another.
And you were there on that glorious day,
Your eyes and teeth sparkling like the sun at noon,
Risen over buildings and mountains to its zenith.
You spoke with a voice as celestial as a guardian angel,
"Did you find anything useful here?"
Yet nothing I beheld had really caught my attention so much as you.
At that moment, I realized I would love mostly
to accompany you anywhere at all,
That anywhere you might yet go, the sun would shine brightly,
Even penetrate the darkest of clouds,
That storms might come and go,
But we might yet
Kindle a fire in our hearts,
A flame of love and tenderness,
Like puppies, like babes,
Like tender shoots of grass and buds on branches,
So are the ends of our fingertips first touching.
That love is now and forevermore.
We are all inseparable,
Even though many miles apart and now generations too.
Where has the time gone?
I remember and dream (and so do you?)

Printed in the United States
By Bookmasters